CHAPTER 2

The man down the snowy slope didn't move.

He can't hear it yet, thought Jesse, and wasn't surprised. Her hearing was extra-sensitive.

A black helicopter flew over the top of the mountain and the sound became louder.

It could have been a pilot flying skiers to untouched slopes, but she didn't think so. Her instincts screamed at her to hide. But there were no trees on the slope, no shelter. She hoped the sun's bright reflection off the snow would make it harder for the pilot to see.

Rotor blades whirring, the helicopter flew closer.

The windows were tinted so Jesse couldn't see who was inside. Aware that a moving target was harder to hit, she skied left, right, then left again.

Steadily, the helicopter circled, like a mosquito about to sting. Small missiles were attached to its sides. Jesse's back muscles stiffened as she anticipated the helicopter shooting at her. It circled again and flew over her head, towards the top of the mountain.

Jesse struggled to keep her balance. It was hard to ski downhill, watch where she was going *and* keep an eye on the helicopter.

There was an explosion, a flash of red.

The people in the helicopter had not fired at Jesse or the mysterious man. They had aimed for the top of the slope.

Jesse heard an enormous growl, as though a giant dog was behind her. There was a crack, and another.

Suddenly, she felt sick. She knew what was happening, even before she looked back one last time. A wall of snow was plummeting down the slope towards her. The helicopter's missile had started an avalanche.

UNDERCOVER GIRL #5:

TWISTED

Christine Harris

WingSpan Press

Printed in the United States of America

Published by WingSpan Press, Livermore, CA
www.wingspanpress.com

The WingSpan name, logo and colophon are the trademarks
of WingSpan Publishing.

ISBN 978-1-59594-151-0

First edition 2007

Library of Congress Control Number 2007924880

CHAPTER 1

Jesse Sharpe swerved to a stop on her skis. Snow shot over her boots. Trying to ignore the rapid beating of her heart, she looked back over her shoulder. Then, carefully, she scanned the white mountain slope in front of her. Left to right. Then back again.

There was no sign of the mysterious man she was to meet. He was late.

Jesse felt a shiver, and it wasn't from the cold.

Her assigned partner, Liam Heggarty, should be meeting this man. But Liam was nursing a twisted left ankle. Yesterday, a skier who had learnt to take off, but not stop, used him to break her downhill run. Liam wasn't badly hurt, but he couldn't easily ski.

Jesse stared at the towering peaks around her. This place was secluded and quiet. She imagined herself skiing across the slope and away, to freedom. She'd have a head-start if she fled now. But the C2 organization would be ruthless in searching for her. If they found her, they would drag her back to headquarters, or make sure that she disappeared for good. They wouldn't want their enemies getting hold of one of their living experiments and finding out the reason for her enhanced abilities.

Erasing thoughts of freedom, Jesse sighed. She would never run away without Jai and Rohan, her adopted brothers. And now there was Tamarind to think about. Besides, Jesse was tied to C2 in a way that few people could imagine.

She rested her ski poles against her legs, propped her sunglasses on top of her head and took a tiny pair of binoculars from her pocket. Then she put the binoculars to her eyes and focused the lenses.

Further down the slope, a dark figure on skis waited, motionless.

There he is.

Returning the binoculars to her pocket, Jesse pulled down her sunglasses. Gripping the ski poles, she bent her knees and took off down the slope.

Seconds later, above the sound of the cold wind whipping her face and her skis sliding on the snow, she heard a disturbing sound that sent warning prickles across the back of her neck.

CHAPTER 3

Jesse's heart pounded. She couldn't reach the side of the slope in time. Nor could she ski downhill faster than an avalanche.

Down the slope, the man in dark clothing also began skiing. Jesse hoped he wouldn't fall over. He looked wobbly.

The sky dimmed.

Automatically reacting to her survival training, she knew there was only one thing to do. Swim. If she moved her arms and legs she might stay near the top of the snow wave. And perhaps she could move to the side, where the snow would not be so deep.

She threw aside her poles and detached the skis, with barely a second to spare. A monster of noise and cold snow knocked her off her feet. It wrapped around her, pressed, scraped and swept her along in its path.

Jesse struggled to keep her head upright.

Although her instinct was to get more air, she clamped her lips shut. Otherwise the snow could fill her mouth. Her body heat would melt the snow and it would flood her lungs. Then she would drown.

A chunk of ice hit her leg. Snow covered her head, spun her round. It seemed as though the frozen skidding and tumbling would last forever.

Then, at last, the avalanche slowed. Jesse cupped her hands over her mouth to create an air pocket.

Memories of being locked, alone, in a dark room in the C2 laboratory came to haunt her. She was about eight years-old at the time. It was a sensory deprivation experiment. The scientists wanted to see how she would cope when she couldn't see or hear anything. Even now, nightmares of that time sometimes woke her at night and she had to turn on the light.

Enclosed spaces brought back those dreadful feelings. In her room at C2, she refused to have a closet. That would mean a dark space behind the doors.

And now she was trapped in darkness under tons of snow.

CHAPTER 4

Jesse couldn't wait for the snow to stop altogether before trying to get free. Snow could quickly freeze hard. But, dizzy and disorientated, she felt unable to move.

'Don't think about what's happened,' Jesse whispered to herself, 'Just work out what you have to do.'

Her hunched body had made a pocket in the snow, so she had air. Although she stored oxygen in her bloodstream for longer than most people, if enough time passed without it she would die. She could be poisoned by the carbon dioxide she breathed out. If she didn't freeze to death first.

I have to calm my breathing. Then I'll use less oxygen.

Grand Master Kim, her martial arts instructor, had taught her, 'Breathing should be silent and deep.'

As she inhaled, she lifted her tongue to the roof of her mouth. She allowed the air to fill her lungs, expanding her abdomen as much as she could in such a cramped position.

'A focused mind is as important as a fit body,' was another thing that Grand Master Kim often repeated. 'Clear your mind of unnecessary noise.'

Jesse imagined the energy in her body was a warm liquid flowing through her veins. She inhaled, then exhaled. And again, several times. Her breathing steadied and so did her heart rate.

She was ready to start digging. But the avalanche had tumbled her over and over. Trapped in heavy snow, she had no idea which way was up. If she dug in the wrong direction, she would be making a deeper hole in which to die.

Quickly, she removed her left glove. She held out her hand, palm up, and spat on it. She felt nothing. Just to make sure, she removed the other glove and patted her palm. *It's dry.* Gravity would draw her spit downwards. Although she didn't feel as though she was upside down, she knew her senses were deceiving her.

Sliding her wet gloves into her pocket, Jesse wriggled and clawed a somersault.

Again, she spat into her hand. This time, she felt warm moistness hit her palm. *Strange, now I feel upside down and I'm not. But before I was upside down, and I didn't feel it.*

She put her gloves back on, then scraped at the snow. The gloves protected her hands a little. But they were not made for digging snow, and her fingers quickly felt numb.

Jesse thought of her C2 partner, Liam. How long would it be before he realised that something was wrong?

CHAPTER 5

My communicator! thought Jesse. Desperate to dig her way out of the suffocating snow, she had overlooked a possible means of getting help.

Her communicator looked like an ordinary watch, but it was much more. It linked her to Liam through text or voice. She hoped it still worked. It might have been shielded by the sleeve of her padded jacket.

Although she had sharp night vision, there was no light at all. She could see nothing.

With cold fingers, she felt for the buttons on her communicator. The letters for text messages did not illuminate. Maybe voice messaging still worked. She pressed that button.

Jesse had no idea how deeply she was buried. Even if the communicator wasn't totally broken, the signal might not be strong enough to reach Liam from underneath the snow. She sent a fervent wish as she pressed the voice button – *Please answer.*

Despite the freezing temperature, Jesse

felt herself break into a sweat all over as she waited to hear if she had contact.

There was crackling. A hiss. That was all.

Her hopes wavered.

If she couldn't dig herself out, Liam was her only chance for survival. He was the one person who knew she was on the north slope. She doubted the mysterious man had survived. Judging by the way he skied, snow activities were not on his list of skills.

Then she heard a voice from her communicator; weak and fuzzy, but definitely familiar.

Pins and needles ran down her arms. 'Liam!'

His words cut in and out.

Desperate, but trying not to sound like it, Jesse kept her voice low and firm, 'There was an avalanche. I'm trapped. North slope.'

She paused, listening for his response.

His voice was furry, a muffled line of sound that made no sense. But even hearing that made her feel less alone.

'Liam?'

The crackling and hissing stopped as the communicator died.

CHAPTER 6

Jesse hoped that Liam had heard her and understood.

However, even if he was on his way, it would take time to search. Time she might not have. After half an hour, someone who was buried by an avalanche had only a small chance of surviving. Most survivors were dug out within fifteen minutes. Jesse knew she had to keep tuneling towards the surface.

She'd read that when people were about to die, their lives sometimes flashed in front of their eyes. But it wasn't that way with her. It was the life she had *not* had. The family she'd never known. She recited the names in the top secret folder that Director Granger had briefly allowed her to see. Since then, she had hoped that one day she would meet her family. Evelyn, her grandmother. Harris, her grandfather. And Chelsea, her identical twin. *She'll look like me. Maybe she'll speak like me too. But she'll live in a proper house, have friends and go to school.*

Jesse was glad that her sister had not been

brought up, as she was, in a secret organization that conducted experiments on people, then sent them out on dangerous assignments.

Time ceased to matter as she dug methodically. Jesse reminded herself that she was unusually healthy and strong, and that some people had been found alive in snow after hours had passed.

She counted to five hundred, then tucked her hands under her armpits to warm them. Then she dug for another count of five hundred. She didn't want to risk frostbite and, if she got out, amputation of the ends of her fingers.

Suddenly she stopped and listened hard. *Is that a noise from outside?* It didn't seem so dark in the snow cavity. Or was she imagining things?

Something sharp touched her left shoulder.

'Owww.' She grabbed it and tugged. *It's a snow probe.*

Overhead, she heard muffled voices, followed by scraping. *Liam!*

Then her elation waned. The memory of the menacing black helicopter, the reason she was trapped, came back to her. What if her rescuer was not Liam, but her attackers?

CHAPTER 7

Sunlight momentarily blinded Jesse. Hands grabbed her wrists and arms. Voices boomed around her, but she couldn't take in what they said.

Jesse detected musky aftershave. *Liam is here.*

She opened her eyes. A group of men surrounded her. They smiled, showing relief that she had been found alive. Someone wrapped an insulation blanket around her shoulders.

Liam limped forward, frowning. He wasn't much to look at, with his pale pock-marked face and spiky hair. But Jesse was delighted to see him.

'Are you all right?' he asked, sounding unusually flustered.

Jesse nodded. 'But you should stop that, you know.'

'What?'

'Frowning. It takes 200,000 frowns to make one wrinkle and look how many you've got.'

Liam raised one eyebrow. Usually he batted

a smart comment back at her, but this time he let it pass.

Jesse noted where the rescue team stood. In any threatening situation, the first thing to do was check out the position of the other people. She couldn't afford to be caught off-guard. Her legs trembled as they struggled to keep her upright. Liam couldn't walk properly with his bad ankle, and he didn't yet know the avalanche was not an accident. So the pair of them were vulnerable.

There were ten men and a search dog, a border collie. Off to one side, where the snow was still thick, snowmobiles were parked at various angles. Each man wore a padded red jacket and had a first aid kit strapped to his waist. Jesse couldn't see any suspicious body language or facial expressions. She felt herself relax a little.

'Miss.' A man with a drooping moustache touched her elbow. He wore a chullo hat with a pattern of tiny skiers around the brim. The chullo hung down each side of his face like knitted ears. 'My name's Paul. Do you hurt anywhere?'

'No. Well, yes. But just bruises.'

'Glad you're okay. We'll take you back to town to see a doctor.'

Instinctively, Jesse stiffened. The word *doctor* meant a lot of things, and feeling better was not one of them. Besides, she had no broken bones and her body would already be healing minor damage.

Pretending to rub some warmth into her face, she moved so that Paul was forced to let go of her arm. 'I don't need a doctor,' she said, firmly. 'And someone else is buried further down the slope. I saw him just before the avalanche. I'm not going till we find him.'

Paul looked surprised.

Jesse stood her ground, with a determined look, and said nothing else. In any negotiation, the first person to speak was the most likely to give way.

At first, Paul looked troubled. Then he shrugged and turned to his companions, 'It's not over yet, boys.'

Another man, wearing a red beanie that was pulled down so low it concealed his eyebrows, peered into the hollow in the snow. 'Where's your cell phone?'

'Lucky you had it with you, Jesse,' said Liam quickly. 'Otherwise we wouldn't have known what happened. The signal was terrible. I'm surprised it worked at all.'

Liam's cover story was sensible. Jesse couldn't tell her rescuers that she had used a secret communicator disguised as a watch.

'I ... lost the phone when I was digging,' she said. 'It was cheap junk anyway. Let's find that man.'

The mystery skier was still buried, and so was his secret. If someone was willing to kill him to stop him talking, then what he knew must be important.

CHAPTER 8

Jesse sat back on her heels, holding the silver insulation blanket close around her body.

Spread out in a line, the rescue team probed the snow debris with long, light-weight metal poles.

The border collie search dog, Thor, ran up and down, his nose to the snow. Jesse's own ability to detect scents was far more developed than in ordinary people. But search dogs were in a class of their own. Thor was sniffing for human scent through deep snow.

Jesse checked her watch, then remembered it was no longer working. But even without knowing exactly how long the mystery man had been buried, she felt the urgency of his time running out.

Side-lined by his injured ankle, Liam stood, arms folded, beside Jesse. His fingers drummed on the sides of his jacket, making a sound like rain on a roof.

Jesse looked up at him. His flat nose leaned to the left, as though it was searching for a better place to lie down. She was sure that he'd once broken it. 'Your ears and the tip of your nose are red from the cold.'

'I've been told my nose is cute,' said Liam.

'People lie.'

He curled his lip. 'Sure you don't want to go back to see the doctor, Thumb-sucker?'

'I'm okay.' Jesse shifted position, wincing when her bruises complained. 'I want to stay.'

Liam nodded as though he approved of her choice.

It wasn't just the man's safety that kept Jesse here, or fear of Granger, C2's Director. It was her feeling that she would be abandoning the mystery man if she left now. They had both been swept under the avalanche. She was free and he wasn't. That didn't seem fair. Even though she had no idea if he was a good guy or bad. Sometimes it was hard to tell. People could be a mixture of both.

'Bad luck about the avalanche,' said Liam.

'Not bad luck,' she said quietly so that only Liam could hear. 'It was good shooting.'

Liam's eyes widened.

She explained about the black helicopter.

Liam looked aside, but not before Jesse saw how much her words had affected him. It surprised her. Liam was adept at keeping his feelings to himself.

'Someone wanted your deaths to look like an accident,' he said. 'Bullet holes lead to questions.'

The search dog began pushing his head into the snow, then started digging with his front paws. Antonio, his handler, watched with careful interest. Both man and dog were scarily alike, big and hairy. Antonio's face was half-obscured by a bushy blond beard.

'Thor's found something!' he called out.

The rescuers picked up their shovels and began to clear snow. Deeper and deeper they went, making a small downhill slope of their own so they could climb in and out of the snow pit. Jesse wondered how far they would go before they gave up. If the mystery man could not be found, his body would have to stay here, frozen, until the spring thaw.

Suddenly there was colour in the white snow, the fringed ends of an orange scarf.

A buzz of excitement ran round the group. The men flung down their shovels and scraped with their hands. Loose snow flew up behind them.

Jesse and Liam moved closer.

As the rescuers dug, the end of a ski appeared in the snow. A foot was attached to it. A leg clad in black ski-pants.

Silently, Jesse nodded to Liam. She recognized the man's clothing. This was their contact. His other leg was bent at a strange angle. *Broken, in more than one place.* Jesse shuddered. *That could have been me.*

Antonio rapidly pocketed his wrap-around sunglasses and flicked snow from the man's face. Blood stained the corner of his mouth and there was a bruised swelling on his forehead. He was in his thirties. Dark-haired, with long eyelashes, and he had a soul-patch on his chin.

The rescuers fell silent.

Gently, Antonio took off his gloves and placed his fingertips under the man's jaw. 'He's got a pulse. It's weak and irregular, but it's there.'

Suddenly the man's eyelids fluttered open. He blinked in the sudden light, as Jesse had done.

She gasped. Although Antonio had announced the man had a pulse, it was like seeing a dead person come to life.

He stared blindly. Then, unexpectedly, the man focused on Jesse. His pupils widened as a shocked expression swept his face. Then fear.

CHAPTER 9

Jesse and Liam stood on the steps of the lodge. The sky darkened as the sun sank behind the mountains. Snowflakes floated downwards, illuminated by the outside lights.

Paul had let them out of his van at the lodge's back entrance, without fuss.

'My niece is shy,' Liam had said.

If I'm shy, then Liam is gorgeous, thought Jesse.

Although she was safe and unharmed, her mind was still on the north slope. Transfixed by the fear on the mystery man's face, she had watched him take a deep breath, then sigh. The fear washed from his face and he appeared to relax. She waited for him to take another breath. But he didn't. His injuries must have been too severe.

'Are you sure you didn't know the dead man?' asked Paul. 'He didn't carry identification. He wasn't a local. None of us knew him. And he wasn't staying at the lodge.' Paul's eyelids drooped with tiredness. Snowflakes were settling on his moustache like bad dandruff.

Jesse shook her head. She knew better than to offer information. Not that there was much to tell. The mystery man had a secret, and he also knew about C2. How did someone find out about a top secret organization that operated behind the front of an insurance company? Even members of the government were not aware of C2. Or, if they were, they never spoke of it in public. Not only that, the mystery man was clever enough to make contact.

Slipping out of the warm jacket that Paul had leant her, Jesse handed it back and shivered as a draft tickled her neck. 'Thank you, for everything.' Deliberately, she smiled and kept her arms loose and relaxed-looking. But inside, she was wound up like a coiled spring.

She sensed a similar disturbance in Liam.

'Get something to eat, young lady, and rest up. This is your lucky day, surviving an avalanche with no major injuries. It happens sometimes. You weren't buried too deeply, or for too long, so that helped,' said Paul. 'What were you doing out there on your own, anyway?'

Jesse's sense of caution took firm hold. Paul could simply be concerned about sensible skiing and saving lives, or he could be luring her into saying more than she should.

'It was beautiful out there, and I went further than I realized.'

'Well, next time, take a beacon.'

'I hope there won't *be* a next time,' she said, with total honesty.

Paul nodded agreement. 'The police will be along in about an hour to ask you a few questions. It's necessary because someone died. No need to worry.'

Actually, there are lots of reasons to worry. She put one hand to her forehead, then allowed her shoulders to droop, giving the impression that she was ready to keel over at any moment. Her recovery couldn't be too quick or Paul would wonder why.

He took the hint about leaving and shook hands with Liam. 'Look after her.'

'I will.' Liam's voice was strange. There were other meanings hidden below his words.

Jesse watched Paul leave, then straightened to stand tall.

Liam muttered, 'Time to disappear.'

CHAPTER 10

Back in her room at the lodge, Jesse picked up a can and began to spray the door handles, taps and anything else she had touched. C2 had all kinds of gadgets, only some of which they let her use. This new spray, which looked like a can of deodorant, dissolved oils left behind from skin, erasing fingerprints.

She wished the C2 laboratory would produce something that smelled better. Maybe other agents didn't notice the odd combination of chemicals. Jesse detected more aromas and sounds than most people because of the nanites in her body. One nanite was thousands of times smaller than a full stop at the end of a sentence. She couldn't see or feel them, yet they were programmed to enter her cells and stimulate her memory and mind power, among other things. Her nanites were busy, traveling 60,000 miles through her body every day.

Jesse glimpsed her reflection in the mirror. Her brown hair, freshly washed, looked shiny under the bathroom light. A thick fringe hung over her eyebrows. When she got back to C2, her carer, Mary Holt, would dive for the scissors. Mary was only happy when she was snipping hair, pushing vitamins or lecturing about healthy eating. And then there was the snooping.

There were shadows under Jesse's light brown eyes. But she didn't look as bad as she feared. *Okay but tired, is my diagnosis.* Her muscles were sore from the pounding her body had taken by the avalanche. But it didn't hamper her movements.

Abandoning the bathroom with nervous speed, she emptied the fruit-and-nut bar wrappers from her pockets into her backpack. Then she grabbed her clothes from a drawer and shoved them in the pack next to the plastic bag containing her wet skiing outfit.

Jesse cast a keen look around the room. She travelled light, so it didn't take much to remove traces of her presence. One final blast of spray cleaned the surfaces she had touched in the bedroom.

She shouldered her backpack, tugged down her sleeve so the fabric covered her hand and opened the door without making skin contact with the handle.

The corridor was clear. Moving lightly, almost silently, she headed towards the lifts. As she passed guest room doors, she picked up clues about the occupants: *Loud cartoons - they've got kids. Coffee – Columbian beans. Sweet perfume, probably French – someone's getting ready to go out.*

A hot shower had made Jesse feel better, but it was too quick. She would have preferred to soak in a hot tub for an hour. Unfortunately, there was no time for that.

Her stomach rumbled and she felt light-headed. *If I don't get some food soon, I'll grab the nearest bunch of flowers and munch them.* The high energy fruit-and-nut bars had hardly greased the sides of her stomach. There was a lot of empty space still in there.

Liam was not at the lift doors yet. His bad ankle might be slowing him down.

Jesse leant against the wall and closed her eyes. She couldn't remember ever feeling so tired.

The sound of rotor blades fills my ears with noise and my mind with dread. I can't see who is inside.

Jesse tried to block the memory of the menacing helicopter. The images were vivid. She almost felt the wind on her face, saw the glint of sunlight on the black sides of the helicopter.

Footsteps told her that someone was approaching.

It wasn't Liam. The steps were too quick and light. Liam trod more heavily. And because of his ankle, he now had a limp.

Jesse opened her eyes. She saw a young man, maybe four or five years older than herself.

He smiled, revealing dimples that would look cute on a three year-old. But the young man's jaw seemed too square for childish dimples.

And there was a shadow on his cheeks and chin that suggested he needed to shave.

A guy like this has no right having dimples, decided Jesse. Then she censored her thoughts. It didn't matter what he looked like.

Thinking he was about to enter the elevator, she stepped away from the door.

But he didn't press the button. He kept looking at her, as though he expected her to say something.

Adrenalin started her heart pumping faster. She looked past him along the corridor, and then behind. This could be a trap.

CHAPTER 11

Except for the two of them, the lodge corridor was empty.

'Have a good day?' he asked.

His voice made her think of honey.

Did he know she was caught in the avalanche? No, she doubted it. Word would have spread through the lodge that *someone* had been trapped. But no-one here knew her. She had kept a low profile. And Paul discreetly dropped her and Liam at the back door so they could slip inside without fuss. This guy wouldn't know it was her at the centre of the rescue drama.

And if there was a threat in what he said, it was so heavily disguised that it was useless.

Perhaps he was just being polite.

She played for safety and acted as though the events of the day had not happened. 'I'm okay,' she said, then added a reluctant, 'Thanks.'

He was standing too close, *way* too close. His right thumb was hooked casually in the belt of his jeans. 'Just had a shower?'

She blinked with surprise.

'Your cheeks are all pink, like you had the water too hot.' He sniffed gently. 'Your hair is still damp and smells of lemon grass shampoo.' His brown eyes were soft and large like those on a home paddock cow.

'Excuse me?' Usually, three or four answers to any question ran around inside Jesse's head. But not this time.

'Am I right?' He lifted one eyebrow.

Whether he was right or not was not the point. When she showered and what shampoo she used were nobody's business but her own. She didn't even know this guy. But at the back of her mind, there was a small but insistent thought that she was glad she had washed her hair.

Jesse folded her arms. 'I'm just starting to realise the research is true.'

'What research?'

'That relative to its size, the tongue is the strongest muscle. And yours is getting a good workout.'

He threw his head back and laughed.

Jesse was glad to see that he had one crooked tooth. Like a fence with one paling out of alignment. It made him seem less like a photograph on the cover of a magazine and more like a real person.

'I have something for you.' He reached into the right pocket of his jeans.

Jesse balanced her weight equally on both feet, ready to spring forward. The backpack gave her free hands with which to defend herself if he attacked. Her eyes narrowed warily as she focused on him.

But all he took out was a small sheet of folded notepaper, which bore the company logo of the lodge.

'What is it?' she demanded.

'Something you'll want to have.' His eyes lit up with silent laughter.

'Do you always speak in riddles?'

'Do you always answer a question with a question?'

It seemed as if they were both talking about completely different topics, although they were in one conversation.

The young man held out the paper.

Probably she shouldn't take it. She should tell him to get lost. But her hand didn't listen to her mind. It moved without permission to take the folded paper.

He looked at her quizzically, with his head tilted to one side.

She wished she knew what he was thinking.

The click of a door lock, then mismatched footsteps – one heavy, one light – warned Jesse that someone else was now in the corridor behind her.

She looked over her shoulder.

Liam, a bag in each hand, limped towards her with a face like an impending thunderstorm.

CHAPTER 12

When Jesse turned back a few seconds later, the young man had gone. He left behind the aroma of new jeans and a pure wool sweater.

She stepped left and peered down the stairs that were next to the elevator doors. But the stairs wound around as they descended and only a few steps were visible. The remaining levels were blocked.

It was odd, but not completely weird. She sighed as Liam drew close. *I'd run if I saw a face like that coming towards me.*

He rested one bag on the carpet and pressed the elevator button. 'Who was that?'

Jesse shrugged. 'I don't know.'

'I asked you a question.'

'And I answered it.' Annoyed with his tone, she closed her hand, concealing the folded sheet of paper.

The elevator doors opened, revealing a middle-aged couple.

Liam and Jesse joined them, standing on opposite sides.

The woman's face was so heavily made up that she could have been spray-painted. Her nails were obviously fake. Bears naturally grew claws that long. And a bear, despite a handsome appearance and soft fur, would rip off your scalp with its claws if it felt threatened.

The middle-aged man half-smiled, without aiming it at anyone in particular. His hair was the equivalent of her nails – too long and too fake. His comb-over started above his left ear and finished at his right.

At last the elevator stopped at the ground floor and the doors opened. It took only a few seconds for the couple to exit. But it was enough for Jesse to see Trouble with a capital T.

Instinctively she moved back, reaching out to jab the 'close doors' button.

Two police officers, one short and stocky and the other tall with red sideburns, stood at the reception desk.

'They're early,' she whispered to Liam. 'Paul said they'd take an hour.'

The doors began to close. But not soon enough.

Behind the counter, the hotel manager saw her. Jesse watched the expressions that chased each other across his face – recognition, surprise, then relief. The manager raised one arm and pointed towards the elevator.

CHAPTER 13

Down in the basement car park, Liam put on surprising speed for someone with a twisted ankle. It was a kind of hop, limp, hop, limp, accompanied by muttered words that Mary Holt would probably ban.

Liam pressed the button on his key ring. The lights on the car flashed twice to show it was now unlocked.

'Get in,' he barked. 'We don't dare get stuck in a police investigation. For all we know, they've discovered it was no accident.'

He dropped his bags in the car trunk and slammed it shut.

Jesse shrugged off her backpack and placed it on the back seat. Her left eyebrow started twitching. She pressed one finger against it and it stopped.

Liam turned the key and accelerated.

Predicting he would launch the car in a screech of brakes, Jesse was surprised that he drove quietly.

'You're driving like a normal person,' she

said, hoping some glimmer of humor was still somewhere inside that grumpy exterior.

'Don't want to attract attention.' He spun the wheel to the right, following the signs that pointed to the exit.

She noticed that he didn't argue that he *was* normal. Liam had no nanites in his body as she, Jai and Rohan did. But he certainly wasn't the same as other people. He was grumpier, for a start.

'So, I'll ask you again, who were you talking to at the elevator?'

She looked sideways at him. 'I don't know. I told you. He just started talking to me.'

Liam snorted.

'What's that supposed to mean?'

'Mm?'

'The snorting. You sounded like a wounded buffalo.'

'And you know what a wounded buffalo sounds like, do you?'

'I'm a genius, remember?'

Liam snorted again. This time, Jesse ignored him. The conversation was going nowhere fast.

At the exit, Liam braked, lowered the window, then reached out to swipe the card. The barrier arm lifted.

'Slide down out of sight.' Liam reached behind with one hand and grabbed a hat he'd flung there the day before. He dragged it down low over his ears. Then he lifted the consol arm next to him and took out a pair of thick-rimmed glasses. Just those two things, hat and glasses, changed his appearance. It didn't take much. Most people never looked that closely at others. A few alterations could make a huge difference.

Obediently, Jesse moved down so she wasn't visible above the dashboard. Her eyebrow began ticking again. It was hard to say which was worse, being interrogated by the police or going back to C2.

CHAPTER 14

As they drove away from the lodge, Liam didn't speak. He settled into a brooding silence. Jesse knew there was no point asking him what was on his mind. He wouldn't say until he was ready.

Half-dozing, she forgot about her cramped position on the floor and let her mind drift. Her thoughts were not fully formed, only fragments of what had happened. She was not asleep, yet neither was she wide awake.

'You can sit up now.'

Liam's voice broke her tired trance.

With one hand, he ripped off his hat and twirled it into the back of the car. His glasses followed.

Jesse wriggled back up onto the car seat. Her legs were still stiff from her tangle with the snow, and her cramped position on the floor had not helped.

Now the car was traveling on a quiet back road.

She yawned behind her hand. But her weariness didn't stop her worrying. If the police had checked up on her background, what would they have found? A girl that did not exist. Not on paper. No parents, no house, no school. And, as far she knew, she was the only other person skiing on the north slope when the man died.

Liam slowed the car down, peering through the windscreen. The snowfall was still light. Hardly snow at all really. More like rain that thought it was cotton wool.

With her vision enhanced by nanites, Jesse could see much further than Liam. She spotted the shape that her partner was seeking. 'He's a mile ahead, parked under a tree.'

When they pulled over to the side of the road, Jesse recognized Liam's battered car. The body work was appalling, but the zippy engine had sped them away from trouble more than once.

A tall, thin man with a grotesque neck got out of Liam's car.

Jesse opened her door, grabbed her backpack and stood up.

Liam limped around to the passenger side of the car. He slapped the waiting man lightly on the forearm. 'Hans, if you get any thinner we can rent you out as a TV antenna.'

So he does still have a sense of humor, thought Jesse, *he's just not sharing it with me.*

'And if you get any uglier, Karate Kate and I can rent *you* out to haunt houses at night.' Hans gave a chuckle which turned into a wheezing cough. His grotesquely thick neck was actually a wrapped scarf.

Jesse smiled. Hans always called her 'Karate Kate'. On her first assignment, she had karate-chopped Hans into unconsciousness in the C2 car park. It had only taken one blow to the base of his neck. Although to be fair, she did sneak up behind him. And it was before she knew he was on the same side. Whatever side it was. She hadn't worked that out either.

But Hans had forgiven her. He almost seemed to like her more because of it. People were strange. *All* people. Not just those with nanotechnology, or who were genetically engineered like Tamarind.

Hans coughed again and it sounded as though he was forcing air through a bag of water.

'That's nasty.' Liam tugged the collar of his jacket up higher.

'Sixty miles an hour,' added Jesse.

Both men gave her strange looks.

'That's the average speed of a cough.'

'She reads too much,' Liam told Hans.

Jesse didn't argue. It wasn't that she read too much. But rather, that she remembered most of what she *did* read.

Liam half-walked, half-hopped to the car trunk to retrieve his bags.

'Has he got a limp?' Hans asked Jesse.

Jesse blinked snowflakes from her eyelashes. 'Yes, he got it on special.'

Hans chuckled.

Liam might be embarrassed if she gave away that a wobbly skier had wiped him out on her first lesson. It wasn't that dramatic. Although the repercussions were. If Liam had gone to meet the mystery man, *he* might have been caught up in the avalanche.

'Any messages?' asked Liam.

'I was just about to tell you,' said Hans. 'The police are on their way to the lodge.'

'On their way?' repeated Jesse.

Hans nodded.

Liam and Jesse exchanged a look that needed no words. Twenty minutes ago when they left the lodge, two men in police uniform were asking for her at the reception desk. If they were not police, who were they?

CHAPTER 15

On the road again, Liam clenched the steering wheel with both hands. An uncomfortable silence stretched into minutes.

But Jesse's discomfort was caused by more than worry. 'I need to eat.'

'Now?' Liam sounded exasperated.

'Yes, *now*. All I've had is fruit-and-nut bars. Do you want me to faint?'

'Uh, sorry. I was thinking ... '

Jesse was tempted to say that he needed all the help he could get, but the look on his face stopped her. Today had been difficult for him too.

It didn't take long to find a large sign with flashing lights that promised good food and fast service. Some of the globes were not working, and the flashing outline made Jesse think of an old man with missing teeth.

The diner door squealed on its hinges when Jesse pushed it open.

If buildings had feelings, this one would be sad. When it was new, it was probably sparkly clean and flashy. Now, fingerprints and red splashes she hoped were misdirected ketchup smeared the walls. Faded green plastic cloths covered the tables. There were only two other customers, seated separately and avoiding eye contact.

Jesse's nose told her the burgers were good. The cook must be better than the décor.

'Yeah?' The young girl behind the counter had a ring pierced into her eyebrow, and she was chewing gum.

After they ordered, Jesse and Liam slipped into a booth beneath the CD speakers. If anyone was eavesdropping with a listening device, it would be almost impossible to pick out their words with loud music playing.

'We can't stop long,' Liam reminded Jesse.

She nodded.

Liam selected a toothpick from a round container. 'Tell me exactly what happened on the north slope.'

Jesse tried to ignore the smell of grilling beef and told him.

'So the avalanche happened *before* you made contact,' he repeated.

'Yes. I saw the man, but he was further down the slope.'

'He recognized you.' The toothpick snapped in Liam's fingers. 'And he was *afraid*.'

'I can't explain it.' Jesse shrugged, wishing she could think of a logical explanation. 'Maybe he was scared because he knew he was dying ... I feel bad about him. He was alive when they dug him out.'

'He was, wasn't he?' Liam sat up straighter.

'If you wanted to make sure that your target didn't return alive, what would *you* do, Ms Genius?'

'Join the rescue party, I guess. But they all looked … right. No-one was acting weird.'

'Do *you*?'

'What? Act weird?'

'You and I go undercover all the time. We're good at it.'

Did he say I'm good at something? The compliment passed in a rush of other words before she could enjoy it.

'Don't you think other people play their parts equally well?' Liam's eyes narrowed. 'Who touched the victim?'

Jesse ran the scene through her mind like a short movie. She remembered a burly, blond man. 'Antonio, the dog handler. But he only felt the man's pulse.'

'Did he? Poison can be administered with the tiniest of needles, hidden in a watch band or ring.' Liam thumped the table.

Jesse flinched. Her earlier sleepiness evaporated. Suddenly she was wide awake.

Liam got to his feet. His chair scraped on the worn tiles. 'Let's change our order to go. We have to find a dead body.'

CHAPTER 16

Slumped in her seat, arms folded, Jesse stared through the windscreen at the lights of the multi-storey building. It had stopped snowing, but her mood had plummeted with the temperature.

'I'm *not* going in there,' she said.

'You went into *Cryohome* on a previous assignment, remember?'

'That was different.'

'Why? Because the bodies were frozen?'

'They were in silver cylinders,' she argued. 'I never even saw a big toe.'

'*Cryohome* don't store toes. Only full bodies or heads.'

She clamped her mouth firmly shut. Seconds ticked by.

'Guess I'll just have to go in alone. I won't have backup, but I'll manage,' said Liam. 'I'll leave you the car keys. If anything happens to me, you can drive to safety.'

Jesse wondered if she appeared sulky, or just plain stubborn. Although there *was* a healthy dose of stubbornness in her refusal, it wasn't that alone. She didn't know what she'd see in the building. A knot had formed in her stomach and it wouldn't go away.

'Look, this is important, kiddo,' said Liam.

Huh. He thinks if he calls me 'kiddo' instead of 'Thumb-sucker' I'll go with him. Well, he can think again.

'I'm worried about leaving you out here in the car by yourself.'

'I'd rather be here than in that building,' insisted Jesse.

'I understand. But somebody deliberately caused an avalanche that could've killed you. Then two men impersonating police officers came to the hotel. Maybe they wanted to find out if our mystery man told you his secret.'

The knot in Jesse's stomach turned to stone. She wished she hadn't wolfed down the burger so quickly.

'If they find you,' added Liam, 'they won't stop at a few polite questions.'

Her mind went places that were worse than the building she could see.

'Are you sure our man is in there?' she asked, grudgingly.

'Hans confirmed it.'

'Can't *he* go in as backup?'

'He's already on his way back to headquarters. Got a message from Granger. Something urgent.'

Guilt rampaged through Jesse. Liam was taking a risk going in there on his own. He really needed another pair of eyes. And somewhere out in that cold darkness, ruthless killers were looking for her.

CHRISTINE HARRIS

'All right, I'll do it,' she sighed.
'Thank you, Jesse.'
'Stop being so polite.'
'Why?'
'It sounds fake.'
'Being polite is fake?' he asked.
'No. Only when *you* do it.'
Liam laughed.

Jesse couldn't help but smile with him. The awkward atmosphere between them forgotten, she felt warmed by the shared joke.

She took a deep breath and peered through the windscreen yet again at the building which housed the morgue.

CHAPTER 17

Under the outside lights, Jesse was surprised by her reflection in the hospital window. In a bobbed black wig, with false teeth over her own, plus a couple of cheek cushions, she looked totally different. *Felt* different. Contact lenses had turned her eyes from brown to a vivid blue. Careful application of eyeliner had subtly widened the shape of her eyes. Wedge-heeled shoes raised her height by two inches.

Her shadowy pursuers were looking for a slim girl with brown hair and brown eyes. They wouldn't look twice at her now. She *hoped.*

The box of clothes, wigs and shoes Liam kept under the false floor in his car trunk was useful. There were gadgets hidden in there too.

She sneaked a look at him. Liam's false beard and bent posture made him look years older.

'There's no way you can hide that limp,' she told him. 'And if we have to run, we're in trouble.'

'We're always in trouble. I'd almost miss it if we weren't.'

Jesse had a bad feeling about this place, this night and the whole situation. But she kept it to herself.

She positioned herself in front of the hospital door. *Why break in when you can walk?* A C2 instructor had told her that sometimes fire-fighters used their *master key*, a sledgehammer, to smash in a door to gain access to a building. Only to find it was unlocked.

Jesse pushed the door and it opened.

Although it was freezing outside, the hospital was warm. Too warm. Her pulse raced and the palms of her hands began to perspire. Beneath the wig, her scalp itched.

On the wall beside the door was a floor plan, with fire exits marked in red. Elevator and stairs were clearly identified. Those stairs led down to the more private areas of the hospital. Jesse stifled a twinge of fear.

Footsteps sounded from the far end of the long corridor. They belonged to a man in a blue uniform. He looked like a hospital employee. His shuffling walk and drooping shoulders advertized that he was tired.

Liam put one arm over Jesse's shoulders and steered her in the opposite direction. They didn't run. Neither did they glance again at the worker. They moved swiftly but casually, as though they were meant to be there.

'There are stairs twenty paces ahead, and then to the right.' Often, Jesse cursed her ability to read and remember. But at times like this, she was glad of it.

The morgue was below ground level. *Just as though the bodies are already buried.* Jesse's mind played tricks on her nerves. Just when she began to feel brave and in control, her imagination interfered. She forced herself to concentrate on their task. 'Liam, if your ankle's too painful, should we take the elevator?'

He shook his head. 'Stairs are safer. We're less likely to bump into anyone. A tired worker will take the easy way, the elevator.'

Jesse said nothing as they made their way to the basement.

There was a silence that was thicker than air. Jesse could feel it. The patients down here did not talk or walk. They would never do so again. Yet she could imagine their voices, feel their laughter and tears.

The corridor was empty.

Two wall cameras, one on the left and the other on the right, were aiming away from Jesse and Liam.

Jesse took a spray can from her backpack and, at a half-run, approached the nearest camera and pressed the button. It only contained cooking oil, but it would grease the lens. Then she did the same with the second camera, hoping no security guard was paying attention too closely.

Together, Jesse and Liam headed for their target area.

The door was secured by a numbered pad where staff would enter the correct code.

Liam slipped a device, the size of a small

cell phone from his pocket. He attached it to the keypad. Nothing happened for a moment, then numbers lit up the screen. 'Bingo.'

He detached the device then punched numbers into the keypad.

The door clicked open.

'Child's play,' he bragged, playfully.

'Huh. No kid would want to come in here.'

Liam hobbled through the open doorway into a large open area.

Jesse felt a rush of heat from the tip of her nose all the way down to her feet. Her skin prickled uncomfortably. The empty corridor, the dull gray of the wall paint, all faded into the background.

Liam glanced back and raised one eyebrow. 'You okay?'

She nodded, hiding her surprise. For now, she'd pretend that she hadn't noticed anything odd. Until she knew the reason for it.

They entered a large open area.

To one side was a closed room with a glass paneled door. Jesse saw silver-colored benches and a large circular adjustable light on a stand. A human anatomy poster, showing arteries, veins and skeletal structure hung on one wall. Human babies were born with over 300 bones. But some fused as the person grew, so an adult had only 206. Jesse's head sizzled with strange facts. They came to her whether she wanted to remember them or not.

A large sink with four taps stretched from one wall of the room to a cabinet with double glass doors. It contained instruments. Jesse averted her eyes. *Don't try and work out what they're for,* she told herself, *you don't want to know.*

On the other side of the open area, Liam pointed to a wall filled with square cabinet doors. The dead mystery man should be lying in a drawer behind one of those doors. To find him, Liam would have to open each one and look.

'Think I'll earn a prize if I guess right the first time?' he said.

She knew he was trying to make her laugh, so she wouldn't be too overwhelmed. But she didn't feel like laughing. Not one bit.

A warning tingle ran across the back of Jesse's neck. Perfectly still, ears tuned for sounds, she held up one hand to signal Liam to be quiet.

'The elevator doors just opened. Footsteps. Two sets, coming this way,' she whispered. 'And they're in a hurry.'

CHAPTER 18

Curled into a ball, Jesse breathed slowly and quietly. *I hope I don't sneeze.*

Today she was unusually glad of her nanites. Anyone who healed at the normal rate would be in a coma by now. Today she had survived an avalanche, seen a man take his last breath, fled from men posing as police officers and crept around a hospital morgue.

Now she was hiding in a rubbish bin. Fortunately, the bin bag was large, strong and new. Suspended from a large metal ring, it had a plastic, pop-up lid. Jesse was concealed all around.

The racing footsteps she had detected became louder.

Were security suspicious about the smeary images on the video monitors, or was this the people who had caused the avalanche and possibly poisoned the mystery man?

He wraps the dangling orange scarf around his neck, once, twice and again. He looks nervous. Perhaps that is why

he's fiddling with the scarf when there is no need.

Another mental picture of the man on the mountain startled her. She decided she was more tired than she realized. And she had eaten very little all day. Her mind was playing tricks.

'How are we supposed to explain *this*?' A voice that probably belonged to a middle-aged man interrupted her thoughts. Jesse imagined him with a deep frown and sagging paunch.

'I … don't know.' The second voice was younger, more uncertain.

'Have you checked thoroughly, Graham?'

Jesse stiffened. A *thorough* check would include looking inside the bin. And in the deep trough where Liam was stretched out. The trough looked spotless and smelled of disinfectant, and the taps didn't drip. But she'd much rather be in the bin.

'I've checked everything. Twice,' replied the younger man, Graham. 'Gurneys, back rooms, and all the fridge drawers.'

'When did you notice something was wrong?' There was a strong note of panic in the older man's voice.

'About half an hour ago.'

'*Half an hour.* What were you doing all that time?'

'I looked for it. Then I had to find you. I haven't told anyone else, not even security. I thought you'd want to know first. Sir, what should we do?'

'Report it to the police.'

'Are you sure?'

'Of course I'm *sure*,' The older man was shouting now. 'A body has disappeared. And not just that, an *unidentified* body. Doesn't that seem suspicious to you?'

Jesse didn't need two guesses to figure out which body. If the mystery man's body had vanished, so had any proof of poisoning. And yet, in a way, it was an answer. Now she was sure the man had been poisoned. He survived being crashed down a mountain under tons of snow only to be caught when he was almost free.

Someone in that group of rescuers, perhaps Antonio, was not who he seemed. Anyone who was so calm and believable when he was finishing off an injured target in front of a dozen people had to be colder than a glacier. That was a truly frightening thought.

Even more puzzling was why they made sure the man was dead, but let *her* live.

CHAPTER 19

The soul patch makes him look like a pirate. Quivering and insecure. But a pirate just the same. He looks surprised to see me. I expected that.

His voice is deep. As he talks, I can see breakfast cereal jammed between his bottom front teeth.

'I made a mistake coming here,' he says.

'Too late for second thoughts,' I tell him.

'Something's wrong.' He looks at me as though he's a plump sheep and I have a knife in my hand.

My heart begins thumping, louder and louder ...

Jesse opened her eyes with a start. She looked up at the four posters of the bed, then across at the telescope near the window. An exercise bike sat, motionless in the centre of the room, between the bed and an orange sofa.

I'm back in the fishbowl. It was hard to think of her tenth floor room in any other way.

Her dreams were disturbing. She saw the man who died on the mountain. It was strange that her mind had made up details like the sound of his voice and the food stuck in his teeth.

Thumping intruded on her thoughts. It came from the direction of the door. Although her dream had been imagination, the sound was real.

Her clothes were crumpled and tainted with the odor of plastic from the hospital bin liner in which she had hidden. There was also a slight tear where the pocket joined the leg fabric of her black pants. She had snagged them during her hurried exit from the hospital. When she finally got back to C2, she had been too tired to change.

There was a fresh round of knocking.

Jesse opened the blinds, then headed towards the door. She looked through the peephole, then undid the locks.

A figure launched itself against her.

Soft arms enthusiastically hugged Jesse.

She hugged Tamarind back, then relocked the door.

Tamarind grinned, showing too many teeth.

Jesse liked that smile. It was full-on. Tamarind had jellyfish genes, but her teeth looked totally shark. Many sharks had five to fifteen rows of teeth. Tiger sharks could produce two and a half thousand teeth in a year. That seemed a lot. But their teeth had no roots like human teeth, so they didn't last long. A week, maybe. A new tooth always replaced the old. If a scientist genetically engineered someone with a few shark genes, they might never have to go to the dentist.

Tamarind's eyes reminded Jesse of the sea. They were incredibly blue. Her flawless skin was unusually pale, almost colorless.

'Focus your breathing,' Jesse reminded her. 'You're starting to glow.'

When Tamarind was nervous or excited, her glowing jellyfish genes kicked in.

'Right.' Tamarind closed her eyes and put her hands together in front of her body. She breathed in, then out.

'What's *that* position called?'

'Standing Zen.' Tamarind answered without opening her eyes.

Jesse couldn't help smiling. Standing Zen was standing loosely, with knees slightly bent. 'That's more like *standing excitement.*'

Tamarind gave up pretending to be calm and grabbed Jesse's hand. 'I was worried about you.'

Instantly wary, Jesse put one finger to her lips to remind Tamarind there were finely-tuned ears everywhere in C2.

A nod showed that Tamarind understood.

'Turn around and close your eyes,' whispered Jesse.

Although Jesse liked and trusted Tamarind, she never showed anyone her secret hiding place. Trusting too much or too quickly was dangerous.

She accessed her secret hiding place and

took out a scanner. In the two days that her room had been empty, Mary Holt could not have resisted the temptation to snoop. *I bet she's planted another bug.*

Moving quickly and efficiently, Jesse ran the scanner over her desk, bed, and the bird kite pinned to the wall. She continued past the small fridge and towards the shelves beside the bed.

The scanner began to flash.

Jesse put it down and felt each shelf. *There it is.* A small hard object, the size of a lentil, was stuck to the underside of a shelf.

Heading straight for her bathroom, Jesse wondered why Mary didn't give up trying to eavesdrop. Perhaps she was testing her. But a lot of C2 listening devices ended up being flushed down the plumbing on the tenth floor.

For now, Jesse slipped the scanner into her pocket. Then she sat beside her friend on the orange sofa. 'All clear.'

Tamarind pouted. 'Reminds me of Nimbus. Only they're worse.'

The organization that had genetically engineered Tamarind and other kids was so ruthless it made C2 look like a charity. And C2 was anything but that.

Anxiety flooded Tamarind's face. 'I was practicing my stretching in the laboratory and I heard something.'

When Tamarind softened her body, it stretched incredibly far. The squelching sound she made gave away her location. She was learning to control that, and the glowing, with the help of Grand Master Kim.

'I was flattened on the floor when the Director and Mary Holt walked past. They didn't see me. I was behind some equipment …'

'You're lucky that no-one treads on you when you do that.'

'Like, totally. I only heard a little of what the Director and Mary were saying. But they were talking about *you*, and it sounded as though something bad had happened. I wish I had your super hearing.'

'Sometimes I hear things that I wish I hadn't.' Jesse tucked up her knees and wrapped her arms around them.

'At least you know what's going on.'

'*Hello.* This is C2. No-one knows what's going on. Anyway, hearing doesn't mean understanding. I just find out how much more I don't know.'

Lots of things had happened on this last assignment that she had not predicted and didn't understand. In the diner when she and Liam were waiting for burgers, he was suspicious of her, bordering on angry. Now, *she* was suspicious of *him*.

CHAPTER 20

Three levels below ground, Jesse stood on the floor panel while her heart rate and weight were monitored. A light beam scanned her retinas.

'Jesse Sharpe, you are cleared for entry,' said a computerized voice.

She walked past the two men on security duty. No point smiling or saying hello. They wouldn't respond. The guards outside Director Granger's office seemed to think that good manners made them look weak.

The door slid open.

As usual, the Director's waiting room was obsessively tidy. Science magazines on a low table were perfectly straight, with all pages in line. *Bet no-one dares pick one up. Moving a magazine out of order would probably mean execution.* That wild idea cheered Jesse for two seconds. Then she saw Prov.

The Director's assistant, Providenza Fellini, seated behind her large oak desk, gave a tentative smile. She reminded Jesse of a puppy, eager for a pat.

Despite Jesse's reservations, she smiled back.

Prov's teased dark hair glistened with hairspray. On anyone else it might have looked old-fashioned. But on Prov, it was stunning. She always wore thick brown eyeliner and bright-colored blouses or fluffy sweaters. Her fingernails were long and painted red. Prov made no apologies for how she looked, and Jesse admired that about her.

In the past, Prov had been kind, giving Jesse snippets of information about her background when she could, and slipping her little chocolates.

Prov had also done other things that were not so good. Although, if Prov had disobeyed her Director's orders years ago, someone else would have been assigned to bring Jesse in.

Many people at C2 had done things they felt uncomfortable about. Including Jesse herself. But she wasn't quite ready to forgive Prov, even though they were becoming less awkward with each other.

Prov fired an urgent look at the Director's closed door, then back to Jesse.

Immediately Jesse was alert. *Is someone in the office with Granger? Someone I won't want to see? Am I in trouble?*

'There's something I have to tell you ...' Prov's urgent whisper was abruptly cut off as the outer door slid open.

CHAPTER 21

Liam entered. His limp wasn't as bad, but it was still noticeable.

He looked from Prov to Jesse, then raised one eyebrow. Obviously, his 'whisper' radar was working.

Jesse smiled in what she hoped was a relaxed, but not overly friendly way. She didn't want to increase his suspicions. But she wasn't feeling that friendly towards him at the moment.

'Prov was telling me how to tease my hair, like hers,' explained Jesse. 'I think it looks cool. I might try it.'

Liam gave a small cough that may have been a suffocated laugh. But he said nothing out loud, just scratched the side of his neck with one finger.

Three ... four ... five, Jesse counted. People showed they were doubtful or uncertain when they scratched their necks like that. And it was usually five times. Exactly.

Prov looked down at her desk, then pressed

the intercom button. 'Director, Liam Heggarty and Jesse Sharpe are here.'

Director Granger didn't bother to reply. He whipped open his door and, with a jerk of his head, invited them both into the interior office.

So it's one of those days is it? Jesse felt her slight hope that this meeting might not go too badly evaporate like morning mist in sunlight.

Jesse stood, without looking at Liam. She sensed he didn't look at her either.

Prov began typing with jerky, rapid stabs of her fingertips. Her long nails didn't slow her down at all.

Granger's office was furnished with only the basics. Not even dust was allowed to infiltrate. Because his office was located underground, there were no windows. Framed maps hung on the walls.

'Sit down.' Granger walked around behind his desk and sat opposite Jesse and Liam. With a long, elegant hand, he smoothed down his tie. His suit was expensive. There was a sheen to the cloth that showed this suit, like his others, was not bought off the rack. It was made by a tailor.

From the corner of her eye, Jesse noticed Liam tapping his foot on the carpet.

Granger pressed his palms together and looked from Jesse to Liam. While some people knew how to hurl insults, Granger knew how to assault with silence. Jesse wondered if he could make people confess to *anything*, even something they hadn't done, just to stop him staring at them.

'I've read your reports,' Granger began in a frigid tone.

Jesse felt a fresh jolt of nervousness. What had Liam written? Did he record his suspicions that the mystery man knew her, that he was *afraid* of her? If she couldn't make Liam believe she had never met the man, she had no hope of convincing Granger. She'd written nothing of her own suspicions about Liam. It was wise not to show her cards until she was ready to play them.

'Liam, you were knocked over by a ...' Granger opened a folder on his desk and appeared to search for a particular reference. 'A learner skier and twisted your ankle. Jesse, you were far more spectacular. You were run down by an avalanche. Which also unfortunately killed our contact. Or, was he poisoned, as you suggest, Liam? But we have no evidence of that because the body was stolen before you could get to it. Oh, and two men pretended to be police officers, but neither of you has any idea about their identities. Does that sum it up?'

Jesse felt as though she was shrinking in the seat. If Granger kept going she'd be nothing more than a little walnut of embarrassed cells.

The Director raised his left arm and rubbed the back of his neck.

Huh. Typical 'you're a pain in the neck' gesture. Granger's body language confirmed what Jesse already knew from his glacial tone. He was irritated.

'We're fortunate that Jesse survived,' Liam reminded the Director.

Grateful that Liam was, in a small way, trying to speak up for her, she felt a fresh warmth towards him. Or was he just trying to make himself look better?

Granger directed his ice-blue eyes towards Jesse. 'C2 is happy when one of the family returns safely.'

Family? The C2 organization was not her family. It was her captor.

'As I have told you before, Jesse, you are precious to us.'

Yeah, right. As a scientific experiment, maybe. Not as a person.

Director Granger frowned. Nothing deep enough to cause unnecessary wrinkles. But visible enough to pretend he was concerned. 'But at the moment, you, Jesse Sharpe, are our biggest problem.'

CHAPTER 22

You've been abducted,' said Granger. What was he talking about? He couldn't be referring to her being taken from the car after the accident that killed her parents. That was years ago. She, Jai and Rohan were all abducted and brought to C2 for Operation I.Q., an experiment in creating child geniuses for undercover work. Granger must mean something else.

The Director opened his laptop, placed his finger on the fingerprint recognition pad, then began to type in his multiple passwords. Just as Jesse did with her own computer.

She glanced at Liam. He, too, looked puzzled. But then, he was a good actor.

'I received this email this morning,' said Granger. 'It says, "We have Jesse Sharpe. We will be in touch soon."' He turned the laptop around.

A video clip started up.

Two men and a girl were walking on a path surrounded by trees. The girl was just in front of the men. She wore an orange jacket, with the collar up around her neck. Her hands were thrust deep into her pockets.

Jesse sat forward.

Both men, wearing hooded tops so their faces were in shadow, sped up and came level with the girl.

Through the camera's eye it was obvious that something was about to happen. The girl didn't notice the men until it was too late.

They grabbed her, one on each side.

The man on her right whipped a small hypodermic needle from his pocket and jabbed it into the girl's wrist.

Then the men spun her around to face the camera, which zoomed in for a closer shot.

She had shoulder-length, brown hair and light brown eyes. Her mouth opened as she struggled to speak. But no sound came out. Already her tongue was paralyzed, useless. The drug they had given her was powerful.

Jesse gasped.

The picture wobbled, then the screen went black.

By then, the silence in Granger's office was electric.

Liam looked at Jesse with astonishment. 'That was *you*.'

CHAPTER 23

No.' Jesse's voice cracked as she answered. 'Someone *thinks* it's me. But it's not.'

'No-one on the whole planet could look that much like you except ...' Liam faltered.

Jesse knew he'd worked it out, but she didn't look at him.

A few months earlier, she had discovered her twin sister's name, *Chelsea.* But seeing her face and hearing the voice that was so like her own, wiped out any pretense that Jesse was calm. 'We have to help her!'

'We don't know where she is, or what the demands will be.'

Jesse leapt to her feet. 'We can't wait for those people to make contact again. Chelsea could be dead by then.'

'Chelsea?' Liam looked even more surprised. 'You know her name?'

She ignored him.

We cannot be sure they really believe it's you, Jesse,' cautioned Granger. 'They may be enticing you into rushing to your sister's side. It could be a trap.'

'I don't care.'

'Well, I certainly do. I cannot let you fall into the wrong hands.'

There was no mention of Granger not wanting her to be hurt. He simply wanted to keep the technology away from others. C2 scientists had done more with nanotechnology than anyone in the outside world suspected. Other scientists only imagined things like healing illnesses or enhancing human abilities with nanites, but C2 had done it.

'On the other hand,' said Granger. 'These people may really believe they have Jesse Sharpe, undercover agent and prodigy. This other girl ...'

'Chelsea,' snapped Jesse. She was past being scared. Past shivering when Granger looked at her. Now she was angry, and determined.

'If they truly believe they have *you,* doing nothing would solve our problem. If you look at it logically, the loss of one ordinary girl would be sad. But the loss of an Operation I.Q. operative, now that would be tragic.'

Liam grunted.

Heat flooded Jesse's face. She was nothing more than a pawn in a game of chess. She had no say over where she would go, who she would chase or run from. A powerful hand made every move. But not this time. 'It won't take them long to find out the truth. They'll do tests and they won't find nanites.'

Granger nodded. 'You're correct, of course.'

Jesse leant both hands on the edge of his

desk and eyeballed him. 'If you remember, I'm good at saving family members. You *owe* me.'

It was a risk, out-facing him like this, defying him. But it was a risk she had to take. She was *not* going to abandon her sister.

CHAPTER 24

Jesse stepped out of Granger's office feeling dazed. Chelsea's face was so like her own. She even wore her fringe in the same way, thick and touching her eyebrows. And yet, there was a different expression in Chelsea's eyes. Not just the fear. It was more than that. Jesse sensed a person who thought and felt differently to herself.

The intensity of her emotions startled her. She had always been protective of her C2 brothers, Rohan and Jai. And, in a way, she thought of Tamarind as a sister. But Jesse's determination to save Chelsea was overwhelming.

Voices hummed behind the Director's closed door. Liam had opted to stay. Apparently, he had something private to discuss.

'Are you all right?' asked Prov.

Jesse looked up. It took a few seconds for her fierce concentration to return to the waiting room.

'I don't know.' Her voice seemed to come from someone else. Someone far away.

Prov got up from her chair and came to Jesse's side. She hesitated briefly, then put one hand on her shoulder. 'Shall I fetch you a drink of water?'

Jesse shook her head.

From behind them, Liam's voice seeped through the door with increasing volume. Jesse hoped he wasn't trying to persuade Director Granger to change his mind about giving her a chance to find her sister. If Liam did that, she would *never* forgive him.

'I'm sorry to lay this on you right now, but I don't know when I'll have another chance,' said Prov. 'You need to be warned.'

That's twice I've heard that now, thought Jesse, *first from Tamarind, and now from Prov.*

Jesse's training kicked in and steadied her rioting emotions. In C2, listening could mean the difference between life and death. She felt her familiar warning of danger, that shivery prickling across the back of her neck, as she listened to Prov's secret.

CHAPTER 25

Jesse knew at a glance that someone had been in her room, although the door was closed. There were several ways of finding out if there had been an intruder. Today she had used the hair trick. She had plucked one long strand from her head, moistened both ends with saliva, then attached it across the crack between the door and the wall. When the door was opened it dislodged the hair.

Ready for anything, Jesse flung open the door.

Mary Holt stood like a startled animal caught in headlights. 'Oh, you surprised me.'

'*You* surprise *me*,' said Jesse.

'I … I'm collecting your clothes for the … to wash.' Mary's frizzy hair made her tiny head seem even smaller.

Mary would be going through every pocket and seam. Not just for tissues or rubbish, but for anything that Jesse might have concealed and forgotten. *Like the sheet of paper that's in the front pocket of those black pants she's got in her hand.*

With all the weirdness going on, and then discovering her twin sister had been abducted, Jesse had overlooked the folded paper given to her by the young man at the lodge.

Moving swiftly, but without looking anxious, Jesse walked towards Mary and slipped the black pants from her hand. 'Thanks so much. Just what I need. Sorry, but I have to get ready straight away. Something urgent has come up.'

Suspicion replaced guilt on Mary's face. 'You've just come back.'

'And now I'm leaving again. Would you mind doing this later?'

Except it wasn't that simple. Typical Granger. He couldn't give a simple *yes* or *no*. He had to make a deal. And Jesse had no choice but to agree if she wanted to help Chelsea.

Mary didn't budge.

Up close, Jesse could see the odd brown fleck in Mary's right eye. Except for that fleck, her eyes were pale green, like grass that didn't see enough sun.

'Granger gets angry when I'm late,' said Jesse.

'*Director* Granger, Jesse. It is not appropriate for you to call him Granger.' Mary clicked her tongue with disapproval.

Jesse couldn't see the difference. Whatever she called him, he reminded her of something slimy that crawled out from under a rock. But she simply nodded. 'You're right. Sorry. It was a long day yesterday.' She tried to look wistful. 'And now they're sending me out again.'

If anything roused Mary to action, it was the thought of duty. She always did hers, made sure everyone knew about it, and admired those who flung the word around as she did. 'Of course. Have you had your iron tonic?'

'No, but I will. I promise. Thank you, Mary.'

If I'm any nicer, I'll have to slap myself. Twice.

Mary snaked her way across the room. 'Be careful,' she said in an almost sincere tone, then closed the door.

Jesse dug in the pocket of her black pants to find the folded paper.

A small object fell to the floor. She bent to pick it up. It was a pink hair-slide. Jesse turned it over in her hand. It must belong to either Mary or Tamarind. She dropped the hair-slide onto the bed, then placed the black pants beside it. With a shiver of anticipation, she opened the folded paper.

CHAPTER 26

Jesse stood in the open doorway of Jai's room.

Too much color or noise disturbed him, so his room was predominantly white. There were no personal items, cushions or books visible. The sparseness of his room suggested that no-one lived in it.

In some ways, Jesse thought, *no-one does.*

Jai sat in a chair, his back to her, facing a computer screen. And yet, his mind would be somewhere that only he could go. He was brilliant, but fragile.

Jesse doubted that Jai could ever go out on assignments, as she and Rohan did. Besides, Jai was insurance that she'd return to C2. Jesse would never leave him. And Rohan would never do it again.

Jai took his hands from the keyboard and rested them on his knees. His wrists were so skinny that Jesse sometimes teased him that they looked like sparrow's legs. His hair had grown longer. It was dark, thick, and as straight as a ruler.

'You have come to say goodbye.' Jai's voice was soft and high-pitched, but he had a quaint way of saying every word carefully that made him sound much older than his nine years.

'Yes.' Jesse took a few steps into the room. 'You know I always see you before I go outside.'

He nodded, but did not turn around. 'It is sensible to do so in case you do not return.'

That was true. But it still jolted her to hear him put it into words.

'You're not going to look at me, are you?' she said.

'I am not.'

She knew, without seeing his face, that the nervous tick beneath his left eye would be visible.

'There is something different about this assignment,' he said.

'I guess so.'

Jai sensed many things that other people didn't notice.

'You are about to do something that is important to you,' he said. 'I deduce that it is personal.'

She didn't answer. Couldn't. Not only was it too close to raw feelings, part of her deal with Director Granger had been that she keep the search for Chelsea a secret. Rohan was on assignment, so that meant less people from whom she had to hide the truth.

'You cannot speak of your mission,' said Jai. 'I understand. However, please take extreme care. This is a place of secrets. We live with them every day. Beware of the rosy apple that has a worm at the core.'

'I have to go now,' Jesse told him. 'They're expecting me in the lab.'

Jai, ignoring his earlier words, spun round on his chair. His dark eyes had the look of a wounded deer who was desperate to avoid the hunter.

CHAPTER 27

Jesse forced herself to lie perfectly still. The slightest movement could blur the image and Michael would have to start the MRI scan again.

She smothered impatience. Every minute she was delayed was another minute of captivity for her sister. But Granger had insisted. In a way, she almost understood.

'You've been through a terrible trauma,' he'd said. 'Being swept away in an avalanche would put most people in hospital. I want you to get a full medical check-up in the laboratory before you leave.' He made sure she couldn't leave until the tests were done. Her palm print authorization to leave the building would not be viable on the computers till noon. But that didn't make waiting any easier.

Although it did give her time to send an email. *I probably shouldn't have done it,* she thought, *but it's too late now.*

Michael had checked her from head to toe, and then some.

'You missed my tongue,' she said, and poked it out.

Michael ignored her. She couldn't insult him. He would've needed feelings for that.

He had taken so much blood for testing that she wondered if he was going to start a blood farm. But instead of milking cows, he could line up patients with one arm stretched out, ready for needles.

Now Michael was taking pictures with the MRI so there was an updated 3-D image of her body on the computer. She'd never seen the finished picture. Could they track her nanites that way?

Despite her earplugs, the loud hammering of the MRI machine echoed through her head. She barely restrained a feeling of panic. Enclosed spaces were hideous and, somehow, she always ended up inside them.

She was glad her nanites didn't react to the massive magnet of the MRI. One time, someone left a pen in the room and it had flown across the room when the machine started up.

Images of the mystery man on the north slope flashed into Jesse's mind. *He's terrified. I smile to reassure him. I just need to get a little closer.*

Confused, Jesse didn't know what to believe. People who had been in accidents sometimes saw the events afterwards in a flashback. But that was something they'd actually seen or done. Nothing imaginary.

I never met that man, Jesse reminded herself.

But now, she was not so certain.

CHAPTER 28

Jesse stepped from the elevator into the C2 car park. Her bike was stored there. Cycling was faster than walking. One day was all that Granger had allowed. *He doesn't care if I find my sister*, thought Jesse.

Her heightened senses alerted her to a presence close by. She sniffed. *A hamburger, and chips.* She checked left, then right.

'How many times do I have to tell you to look *behind* as well?'

She spun round.

Liam wore a cocky grin and carried a brown paper bag in each hand. 'Pickles or no pickles?'

'I'm in a hurry.' She strode away from him.

He followed, still limping.

'What are you doing here?' she snapped.

'I'm taking a sick day.' Hop, limp, hop, limp. Even with his injured-ankle walk, he still kept up with her.

'You don't take sick days.'

'I do when my friends need me. Besides, I'm curious.'

'Why?'

'I want to see your sister. Then I can decide who's better looking.'

'Go away,' demanded Jesse. 'And please stop that stupid walk.'

His eyebrows rose.

She shot him her *you-are-so-sprung* look. 'I don't know what you're up to, Liam. And right now, I don't really care. But I know there's nothing wrong with your ankle. You keep changing sides. You started off favoring your left leg, then you switched to your right. Now it's back to your left.'

He gave a wry smile. 'I should have figured you'd work it out. That's what happens when you're partnered with a genius.' The laughter left his eyes. 'I'm sorry. I promise to explain. Let me help. Please?'

Uncertain, Jesse looked at her partner. If he let her down this time, her sister's life would be at stake.

CHAPTER 29

Liam planted his foot on the accelerator and the car took off with a screech of tires.

I hope I'm doing the right thing, thought Jesse.

'The park is about twenty minutes from here. I recognized the bird sculpture in the background of the video clip,' said Liam.

Jesse had recognized it too, but she didn't say so.

'I jog there,' added Liam.

'You *jog*?'

Liam snorted. 'How else would I get my phenomenal strength.'

'Amazing.'

'My phenomenal strength?'

'No. That you know a word like *phenomenal.*'

He reached out with one hand and gave her a light tap on the back of her head.

I must be on his A-list. He only smacks people he likes.

She took a large bite of the burger, then

spoke with her mouth full. 'This food isn't bribery, is it?'

'Can't fool you Operation I.Q.'s.'

Jesse swallowed hard. 'Then why did you try?'

'Look, this whole situation is a complicated mess. If you find a length of string that's twisted and full of knots, you untangle them one at a time, right? Question for question. I'll answer if you do.'

'Okay.'

Liam braked at the street exit, then turned right. The traffic was light, so they would make good time. 'You first.'

'Why did you lie to me about your bad ankle?'

'Orders from Granger.'

Temporarily, Jesse forgot about her burger. She turned to stare at Liam in amazement. '*Granger* told you to pretend you twisted your ankle?'

'Not exactly. He contacted me at the lodge and told me to find an excuse to stay there. So you would meet our mystery man. I guess I messed up by inventing a sore leg. Limping makes the other leg sore, even if it wasn't to begin with. And then I had to keep it up *and* remember which ankle. As you discovered, that isn't so easy without a computer brain like yours.'

'My brain isn't a computer. It's just improved by computer-controlled nanothingammies.'

'Thingammies?'

'I'm sick of thinking about them.' As the car stopped at a red traffic light, Jesse looked out through the window at a restaurant. 'Someone in there just burnt milk on a stove. See what I mean? There's always a sound, something I see, or a thought that won't go away.' She didn't mention the vivid pictures she was seeing of the man on the mountain, but it worried her. A lot.

'Must be like being nagged,' said Liam, 'Only you're doing it to yourself.'

'Exactly.'

'I told Granger this morning what I thought about his keeping me away from north slope.'

'So that's what the raised voices were about in his office.'

'You could've been killed in that avalanche.'

Jesse had recognized Liam's fury, but not the reason for it.

The car accelerated again. Liam checked the side mirror, then slammed left around a corner.

Jesse slid sideways in the seat.

Liam turned a quick right, then left again. 'Just making sure we're not being followed.'

'Should work. Anyone who drives like this will end up crashed against a wall.'

'So what does that tell you?' he asked.

'That you're a crazy driver.'

'What do you think about Granger keeping me out of the picture on the north slope?'

'C2 is involved.'

'My thoughts too.'

'There's more.' Jesse chose her words carefully. She didn't want to get Prov into trouble. If Granger found out his assistant was leaking information, Prov would be in danger of losing more than her job. 'I was supposed to meet the mystery man at 11 a.m. He was late. It was nearly 11.30 a.m. when the avalanche happened. At 11 a.m. Granger was overhead saying that something terrible had happened on the north slope. That was thirty minutes *before* the avalanche.'

Liam braked, as though he couldn't drive fast and absorb her revelation at the same time. 'Now that's interesting.'

A frightening idea attacked Jesse. 'You don't think Granger arranged to have me killed, do you?'

'No. If it was as simple as *get rid of Jesse Sharpe*, he would've told me to do it.'

CHAPTER 30

Jesse threw an anxious look at Liam.

'Relax, Thumb-sucker,' he said. 'If I was going to remove you, you wouldn't know about it.'

It was strange how people in C2 used nice little phrases like *cleaning up*, *removing*, or even *housekeeping* to describe murder.

Then he added, 'I wouldn't do it, Jesse.'

If he'd been ordered to get rid of her and disobeyed, he wouldn't be here driving the car.

'Besides, a gun is surer than an avalanche. As we've discovered, people survive avalanches,' said Liam. 'Your turn. Tell me about the mystery man on north slope.'

She hardly knew what to think herself, never mind explaining it to Liam.

'Just talk to me.' His voice was gentle and it disarmed her defenses.

'I thought I hadn't met him. But since then, I've been seeing him ... It's not like a dream. It's more like something that I'm remembering, but in bits and pieces.' She pushed the remainder of the burger back into the bag and put it on the seat beside her. Liam's way of rubbish disposal was dropping it on the floor. But she wasn't that influenced by him yet.

'What are you remembering?'

'I didn't have good feelings towards him,' she said, reluctantly. 'I was going to do something ... bad to him.'

'Something bad?'

'I'm not sure. But, he's dead, isn't he?'

'You couldn't kill anybody,' said Liam, in a definite voice. 'I especially don't believe you could kill somebody and not remember it.'

'What if I was brainwashed?'

Liam shook his head. 'I'm not sure there *is* such a thing as brainwashing. You can influence, bribe or threaten people. But making one person murder another and block it out? No. Anyway, when would this have happened? No-one's had time to work on you, have they?'

Liam's ideas were logical and believable. And yet, Jesse knew she wasn't like other people. The nanites in her body made her senses acute, gave her strength and endurance. They helped her body heal amazingly fast. Her mind worked at top speed. And now she wondered if C2 had found a way to make her do things that she would normally refuse, and then wipe the memories? If her fears were true, then C2 had turned her into a murderer.

CHAPTER 31

Jesse and Liam sat in the car and looked across the street at the park.

'You're using yourself as bait,' said Liam. 'You're not in disguise. And that video showed the location so clearly that any dummy could have worked out where it is.'

Jesse felt a flutter of nerves. 'My sister is in trouble because of *me*.' She wiped her sweaty palms down the sides of her jeans. 'You don't have to hang around. This isn't your problem.'

Liam scraped one hand across his chin. He hadn't shaved for a couple of days. 'I can't be bothered showing *another* new partner the ropes. And these people, whoever they are, will expect you to bring me along.' He took the car keys from the ignition. 'I'm curious, though. What do you have over Granger that made him agree?'

Although Liam had helped her on the last assignment with surveillance, he didn't know the target's true identity. 'Everyone in C2 is entitled to a secret,' she said, and got out of the car.

Liam couldn't argue. He had secrets of his own.

Although there was blue sky, the wind was chilly. Jesse was glad of her thick purple sweater.

As they entered the park, the fluttering in her stomach turned to churning.

Quietly, without drawing undue attention to themselves, Jesse and Liam strolled to the bird sculpture. Its bronze wings were outspread, balancing a fat belly. The bird's bulging eyes made it look frenzied.

I know how it feels, thought Jesse.

Surrounding the sculpture was a grassed area, with beds of yellow flowers. Walking and cycling paths crisscrossed from left to right. And behind that, there was a line of thick bushes. The sound of car doors told her a car park was on the other side of the bushes. There were a few walkers and two mothers with baby strollers, who were doing more talking than exercising. But overall, the park was quiet.

'Two o'clock. There's a glint of light in the bushes,' said Jesse. 'Either someone's got binoculars or they're taking photos.'

'I see it.'

It was natural that she and Liam would seek clues. So they poked around in the grass and in bushes.

'They're still watching,' said Jesse. 'They might not try anything with you beside me. Let's separate.'

Liam didn't argue. She expected him to, but he probably knew it would be useless. This was *her* plan. He was only here to help.

'I'll keep an eye on you from a distance. But it's risky. This is a public park. I can't just draw my gun and shoot.'

She grabbed his wrist. 'No gun. I *want* them to take me. Otherwise I'll never find Chelsea.'

'Jesse, that video was emailed hours ago. You can't be sure she's still …' his voice trailed off.

'She's *alive*.' Jesse willed him to believe her. 'Why don't you head to the right? I'll go left.'

Restless and anxious, Jesse walked away from him.

And kept walking.

She glanced at her new communicator watch. It was thirty minutes since she'd entered the park. What if the glint in the bushes was innocent? There was plan A, and then nothing. No plan B.

Mentally, Jesse was transported from the park back to the north slope. *I remove the pink slide from my hair and hit him with it on the strip of bare skin between his glove and his sleeve. The prick of the tiny needle would've been little more than a sting. But the effects of the poison will be much worse.*

Her mind spun with sickening thoughts. *I did it. I poisoned him.* She remembered Liam's definite, 'You couldn't kill anyone.' He was wrong. And there was proof. Not just the memories that were resurfacing, but she had found the pink hair-slide in her room.

Before she could fully absorb her returning memories, Jesse's acute hearing picked up furtive footsteps behind her, moving quickly in her direction. *A man: big build, breathing nervously, he's a smoker and he's recently eaten garlic.*

Jesse's instinct was to scram. But she kept a steady pace. It was like standing in the middle of the street, waiting to be run down.

The urgent footsteps caught up to her.

Rough fabric was thrown over Jesse's head.

CHAPTER 32

Inside the bag, the stuffy air smelled of hessian and old potatoes.

Jesse heard a van door slide open. She was half-rolled, half-dropped into the back of the van. She fell sideways, banging her elbow on the hard floor. *No seats. Must be one of those work-type vehicles with open space at the back.*

The door slid shut.

This wasn't the first time Jesse had been abducted. Although it was the only time she had deliberately allowed it to happen. If her position in C2 was advertized as a regular job, it would include, 'Must be prepared for abduction and welcome bruises.'

She heard the motor start. The van floor vibrations told her the vehicle was moving.

'You can come out. It's safe,' said a young, female voice close by. 'Well, not safe, exactly. But there's only me and you in here, and a wall between us and the goons in the front.'

Jesse felt as though an invisible hand had reached into her chest to squeeze her heart.

She broke out in a perspiration that had nothing to do with the hot, stuffy bag over her head and body. Eager to wriggle out, but petrified to do so, she froze.

'Okay, stay there then,' said the voice. 'Maybe you're one of those people who like having bags over their heads. You can get therapy for that, you know.'

Familiar voice, smart mouth, thought Jesse. *This is definitely my sister.*

'But if you do decide to un-bag yourself, I'd love it if you'd untie my hands. My arms are getting sore.'

Jesse struggled out like a caterpillar leaving a cocoon. As she pulled the bag over head, she felt static electricity tease her hair. *Great. The first time my sister sees me and I'll look like a sea anemone.*

Free of the bag, her eyes were immediately drawn to her sister's face.

Chelsea's shoulders slumped with disappointment. 'Oh. It *is* you.'

CHAPTER 33

You know who I am?' Jesse ran both hands through her hair, trying to tame it.

'*Hello*, looked in the mirror lately?' Chelsea rolled her eyes. 'Can you untie me? We can do the family stuff afterwards.'

Numb with shock and a disappointment of her own, Jesse crawled across to Chelsea. *This isn't how it's supposed to be.* She had imagined tears and hugs.

Chelsea leant forward so Jesse could reach to untie her wrists. 'Those goons drugged me. When it wore off, they let me out to use a bathroom and get a drink of water. That's when they told me that my sister was alive. At first I didn't believe them. I thought you'd died in the car accident. But I see that's not true. Look at your *nose*.'

'What's wrong with it?'

'Looks like a ski jump.'

Jesse undid the last knot in the rope.

'Don't worry about it too much,' said Chelsea, as she rubbed feeling back into her wrists. 'I've got a nose just like it.'

The two girls stared at each other.

'You've got freckles,' said Jesse. Chelsea had been outside in the sun more often than she had.

'You've got longer hair. Did you know about me?'

'I found out a few months back. But ...' She didn't know how to continue. It seemed wrong to start off lying to her sister, and yet it wasn't possible to tell her the whole truth.

Chelsea grabbed Jesse's arm. 'It's okay. Let's get out of here first, then we can have our first argument.'

'Why would we argue?'

'Sisters *always* argue.'

'Do they?'

'Where have you been?' Chelsea made a face. 'Another planet?'

'Kind of.'

'I was so hoping they wouldn't get you,' said Chelsea. 'I don't think they're very nice people.'

The van turned a corner and both girls swayed.

'People who go round abducting other people usually aren't.'

Chelsea grinned. 'Smart, aren't you?'

'More than you know,' said Jesse, dryly. 'What do these people want with us ... me?'

'They took me to make you come charging to the rescue, but I guess you already know that.'

Jesse nodded.

'And you? They're going to sell you to the highest bidder.'

CHAPTER 34

'One of those guys, the boss I think, said they were going to get a lot of money for you,' Chelsea explained. 'Sort of like eBay, but with a person instead of a celebrity fragrance or designer jeans. Would they really get that much?'

'Gazillions.' Jesse could think of a few organizations that would be eager to get their hands on the nanotechnology that was in her body. And she shuddered to think what they would do to extract it, or how they would erase the evidence once they had done so.

However, she couldn't work out how anyone knew about her. It had to be someone from C2. But only certain people understood about the nanites and her enhanced abilities. Unless someone absolutely had to know something, they weren't told. Jesse remembered Jai's comment about a worm hidden inside an apple.

'You're not a movie star or anything, are

you? I would have seen you. I go to the movies a lot.'

'No way.'

'What do we do now?' Chelsea's words were brave, but she sat with her arms folded protectively around her body, and there was an expression in her eyes that showed she was far more frightened than she pretended.

In one quick glance, Jesse saw the back of the van was almost empty. There was a crumpled rug near her sister, but no tools or objects that could be hurled at their abductors.

'I'm going to call a friend.' Jesse pushed back the sleeve of her purple sweater and pressed the *voice* button on her wrist communicator.

Chelsea slapped her right hand against her cheek. 'Oh great. The first time I meet my sister and she arrives with her head in a bag and now she's talking to her watch.'

It's worse than that, Jesse thought, *I could be a murderer.* Even more shocking than the memory of injecting that poor man, was how she had felt at that moment. Nothing. Nothing at all. No guilt, no sympathy.

She dragged her thoughts back to the present.

'This is like a cell phone.' She tapped her wrist communicator. 'Only I wear it on my wrist.'

'Cool. Is it from Japan?'

Jesse shrugged.

Liam didn't answer her call. Had these crazy people done something to him? Already, her sister was caught up in this mess because of her. Jesse didn't want her partner hurt as well. She sent a text message and hoped he would see it.

The van slowed down.

Chelsea's pupils widened.

Jesse wondered if she looked just as fearful. No matter how much training someone had, in a situation like this, it was natural to be scared. But her martial arts training helped her understand that she needed to control her thoughts and turn her fear into strength. If her nerves took over, she couldn't protect Chelsea or herself.

'I can do karate and tae kwon do,' Jesse told her sister. 'And now I'm learning Qi Gong, which also has a martial arts application.'

'Tae kwon do? Isn't that where you run around in a white dressing-gown and throw guys over your shoulder?'

While throwing guys over her shoulder had some attractions, Jesse simply said, 'It's a way of kicking and punching.'

'Do you jump over trees, like in the movies?'

'As if. Some days I'd be lucky to jump over a weed.'

Jesse reached down and slid a tiny object the size of a sewing needle from where it was tucked between the tongue and laces of her sneakers. She opened her mouth and slipped it between her gum and cheek, where it was invisible.

The van stopped.

Chelsea started to speak, but Jesse put one finger to her lips. She needed to listen carefully.

We're in a car park or building. Echoing voices. Two sets of footsteps, approaching the van door.

Adrenalin pumping her heart into faster action, Jesse balanced herself, ready to launch from the van against whoever opened the door. The element of surprise could give her an advantage.

C2 forbade her to carry a gun. Maybe because they thought she'd turn it on someone in the organization. It suited Jesse. She didn't want a gun. One squeeze of the trigger could end somebody's life. And what if, in that split second, the shooter realized that he or she had aimed at the wrong person, or for the wrong reason? It would be too late.

But you didn't need a gun to take a life, as she'd recently discovered.

The van door slid open.

Jesse saw a familiar face. One that she had not expected.

CHAPTER 35

Two men stood well back, their guns aimed into the van. They knew to keep clear, where Jesse couldn't spring out and knock them over.

The tall man on the right gave a deep, juicy cough. Then he said, 'Out, please.'

Disappointed that her idea of a surprise leap was not going to work, Jesse obeyed. Chelsea scrambled out behind her.

'Hans Faulkner,' said Jesse in a tone of disgust. She hoped the tiny device in her mouth would stay tucked along her gum as she talked. And she also hoped that she wouldn't set it off by accident.

Hans gave a mocking smile.

Chelsea looked confused. 'You know him?' She swung back to look at Hans.

'Every human spends half an hour as a single cell,' Jesse said to Hans. 'Looks like you broke that record. You're *still* a single cell.'

'I apologize, but you're my retirement insurance.'

The man next to him had long, red sideburns which Jesse had also seen before.

'Gave up being a police officer, did you?' she said.

'You're right, Faulkner,' he said. 'We *will* get a lot of money for her. If she can keep her mouth shut for two seconds.'

'That's asking a lot.' Jesse threw an inquiring look at Chelsea. 'Don't you think, Sis?'

Chelsea's mouth was open, but no sound came out.

They were in an old warehouse. There were windows, but they were too high up for Jesse to see outside. But they hadn't traveled too far and the sound of trains outside told her that they were near a railway line.

What would Liam say when he found out that his friend and former partner was behind this?

Now Jesse understood how the body disappeared before she and Liam reached the morgue. Hans relayed information to his associates.

Anger sparked inside Jesse. 'If you wanted to grab me, why did you cause that avalanche? That poor man was killed.'

'You were in an avalanche?' gasped Chelsea.

Hans blew air from his lips in annoyance. 'I didn't cause the avalanche. You're worth much more to me alive. Borger was working for me. We were going to bring you in then, but the snow overhang broke off.'

'*Broke off?*' Jesse burst out. 'Someone fired a missile at it from a helicopter.'

'Missile?' Chelsea was beginning to sound like an echo.

'Rubbish,' said Hans. 'There was no helicopter. My men were there. I think they'd know.'

Jesse was mystified. She *saw* the helicopter. Why would Hans lie about it? He had nothing to gain. Did he know that she'd poisoned that man, Borger?

'You took the body from the morgue,' Jesse said.

'Morgue?' Chelsea's tone was creeping higher and higher. 'You went to a morgue?'

'I didn't want any links to me. As they say, if you want something done right, do it yourself. I had to step in and take control.' Hans coughed again. 'This job is wrecking my health. I'll be glad to get out.'

'Your man wasn't poisoned?' said Jesse.

'Poison? Helicopters? What is all this?'

Jesse looked at her sister's face. It was pale and strained.

'Hans, you have me. Let my sister go.'

'I don't like unnecessary violence. I've let several opportunities pass because Liam was there. I would've had to kill him. He was my partner. I've got *some* standards.' Hans sighed. 'Sadly, it is different with your sister. She's seen my face. I cannot let her go.'

CHAPTER 36

Jesse wriggled her nose and blinked rapidly, working up to a loud pretend sneeze. She put her hand up to cover her mouth. With two fingers, she took out the small device she had concealed there.

Slowly, casually, she lowered her hand to waist height.

In a split second, she saw a shift of expression in the eyes of the man with the red hair. *He knows something's up.*

Jesse pressed the tiny button on the device. There was a *phfft* sound. The man's eyes glazed over and he crumpled onto the stained concrete floor. His heart would be pumping tranquilizer through his body.

Hans instinctively looked at his associate.

Now. Jesse flew forward, turning her body sideways to the gun. She grabbed Hans Faulkner's wrist so that he couldn't swing the gun around. Then she slid her hand around and under the gun. She knew better than to position her hand in front of the nozzle. If the gun went off, so would her hand. In pieces.

She pushed down on his wrist with her right hand and shoved the gun barrel up with her left. There was a sickening snap as Hans' thumb broke. The gun clattered onto the floor. Immediately, she kicked it across the warehouse floor into the shadows.

Hans groaned. He was too well trained to scream. But Jesse would bet he was tempted. It wasn't good to hear the snap of his thumb bone. But breaking one thumb seemed a small price to pay for saving two lives. Grand Master Kim had taught her that good intentions were important in self-defense.

Jesse swung around, aiming a hard kick at Hans' right knee. He buckled, almost fell, but regained his balance.

He swung at her with a clenched fist.

Jesse ducked.

She had to be light on her feet, and quick. Despite his broken thumb, Hans was bigger and heavier then she was, and he had been an undercover agent for a long time. It would be foolish to underestimate him.

Her aim was to disable him without doing too much damage. If she fought to kill, she would be no better than him.

'Go girl,' Chelsea shouted. 'I'll get the gun. Then you can shoot him.'

'I don't shoot people,' Jesse shouted back, as she grappled with Hans.

Chelsea dashed past.

Don't get too close. Jesse was distracted by her sister's sudden movement.

Hans shoved Jesse backwards and lunged at Chelsea.

Jesse staggered.

Hans threw his arms around Chelsea. His left arm circled her body, pinning her arms. His right arm curled upwards so that his hand gripped her neck. Hans Faulkner's face was dripping sweat. Pain from his broken thumb scored deep frown marks. 'Don't move,' he told Jesse. 'I don't need a gun to get rid of her.'

Jesse stared at his strong hand on her sister's neck and knew it was true.

CHAPTER 37

Hans ignored the unconscious body of the red-haired man and forced Chelsea across the warehouse floor. 'Don't follow us, Karate Kate.'

Jesse didn't move a muscle. *Where's Liam when I need him?*

She stood motionless, listening to two sets of footsteps, one heavy and the other dragging reluctantly. There was a flurry of wings as their stumbling progress disturbed some pigeons.

Jesse crept after her sister.

The walls of the abandoned warehouse were covered with graffiti. Some was neatly done, in bright colors. But most of it was unreadable scribbles.

She pushed open the dented door, just a fraction, and peeked outside. A cold wind made her shiver. Although her instincts urged her to dash after her sister and drag her away from Hans, she resisted. There was a fierce ruthlessness about him that Jesse hadn't noticed before. If he felt threatened or was too closely pursued, he would carry out his threat against Chelsea.

I can't lose my sister already, thought Jesse. *We haven't had that argument yet.*

Hans glanced back towards the warehouse doorway.

Jesse kept still. Leaping back to shut the door would only make her more visible. She doubted that he could see that the door was slightly open, although he would guess she was watching from somewhere.

Her eyes focused. The nanites did their work and her eyes zoomed in like a telescope. Hans had shifted his hold on Chelsea. He had one arm around her shoulders, hugging her tightly to him. But he could react in seconds.

Chelsea's back was as stiff as a surfboard. She stumbled as she tried to look back. Hans squeezed her shoulders and kept her marching forward.

They climbed the steps of a crossover that took pedestrians safely over the railway tracks.

A noisy family blocked Jesse's view. The mother was dragging a protesting boy up the steps. He wriggled and shouted, but finally the mother won.

Jesse could no longer see Hans and her sister. They had disappeared down the other side of the crossover.

She raced along the outside wall of the long warehouse, then up the pedestrian steps.

Careful now. Don't go too fast. She didn't

want to startle Hans. But neither did she want to lose sight of him and Chelsea.

From the top of the pedestrian crossover, Jesse looked down onto the station.

Hans and Chelsea, in her bright orange jacket, stepped into the fourth carriage. The doors closed and the train began to move away.

CHAPTER 38

Jesse felt a surge of panic.

The train was beneath the pedestrian crossover. There was a bend in the track, so the train was moving slowly. But it would soon gather speed and vanish from Jesse's sight.

Ignoring the passengers coming and going behind her, she looked down. Then she boosted herself up with both arms onto the railing. Her legs swung over the side.

'Hey, you,' a male voice called from behind her.

Jesse didn't look around. *If I miss or slide off the carriage roof, I could be crushed by the train wheels. I have to get it right.* Her nanites and her martial arts training gave her excellent balance. But things could go wrong, and sometimes did.

She counted carriages, *two ... three.*

A hand grabbed her arm. 'Get back up here.'

Four. She pulled free and lunged forwards.

Thump. She landed on the roof of the train

carriage on both feet, then pitched forward onto her stomach.

Wind blasted her face. Grit stuck in her eyes. Her heart went off the scale as she lay, not daring to move, in case the wind blew her from the top of the carriage.

There were no railings to hold. No ladders on the side. It was too dangerous to stand. She would have to crawl or wriggle on her stomach to the end of the carriage where she could lower herself down.

She edged forward.

The train lurched around a bend. She waited till it straightened again before resuming her slow crawl to the end.

Then, still on her stomach, she pushed her body around until she was facing the opposite direction. Stretching out her left foot, she felt blindly for the top rung of the ladder. Her leg swung in mid-air, with nothing to support it. Any bump of the train on a join or uneven bit of track could send her sprawling.

Finally she was low enough to touch the top rung with one foot and wrap her fingers around the railings of the ladder.

Damp with perspiration, she reached the narrow ledge outside the carriage and slumped back against the wall. She let herself rest for only a few seconds. Then she sidled up to the glass panel in the door and peeked inside.

Hans and Chelsea were seated three rows from Jesse. Hans was on the outside, trapping Chelsea against the window. His eyes darted nervously about.

The moment Jesse opened the door, he

would look around. And most likely, someone from the pedestrian crossover had already rung the police. They would put someone on the train at the next station. Or they would ring through to the driver and he'd send someone to find her. She had to move quickly.

CHAPTER 39

Jesse opened the carriage door and hurtled towards her sister's captor.

Hans half-turned. Before he could fully twist around, Jesse chopped the base of his neck. The brachial plexus origin had an artery and several nerves running through it.

'Sorry,' she whispered. 'This is getting to be a bad habit. But you didn't leave me any choice.'

Hans slumped sideways onto Chelsea.

She made a face and shoved him away.

He toppled forward, his head coming to rest on the back of the seat in front.

Although the carriage was only half-full, passengers were staring. A solidly-built man in a gray suit got to his feet.

Jesse held out one hand to Chelsea. 'Let's get out of here.'

Chelsea jumped to her feet. 'Can I tread on him?'

'Please do,' said Jesse.

Chelsea climbed over Hans and jumped down onto the floor beside Jesse.

Hans moaned and struggled to sit up.

Chelsea squealed.

I didn't hit him hard enough, thought Jesse.

Together, she and Chelsea shot through the carriage door onto the narrow ledge outside.

Chelsea shouted above the noise of the train and the rush of wind. 'What now?'

'We jump off the train.'

'No way ...'

Jesse talked over the top of her sister's protests. 'Your jacket will give you some padding.'

Hans appeared at the door, glaring at them through the glass panel. He still looked groggy, but he was fast waking up. And he was not happy.

'Jump out and *away* from the train, so you don't get caught under the wheels,' Jesse told Chelsea. 'Try to land on your side, so you hit evenly.'

'But ...'

Jesse put one hand on Chelsea's back and pushed.

CHAPTER 40

Jesse hit the ground and rolled down the embankment, coming to rest against a prickly bush. 'Ouch.' Chest heaving, struggling for air, she lay still. Everything hurt. Her bones were jarred. She flexed her feet, legs, then moved her arms. *Nothing is broken.*

She sat up and looked along the track. 'Chelsea?'

More nervous about facing her sister than she was about fighting Hans, Jesse scrambled awkwardly along the track. She had wanted to save Chelsea, not injure her.

Cars drove past on the street, oblivious to the drama trackside. For most people, this was just an ordinary day.

Jesse felt enormous relief when she found Chelsea.

Her sister was nursing a sore elbow, and there was a swelling on her forehead. Her orange jacket had a long tear in one sleeve.

'I hope you don't do that to all of your friends.' Chelsea grimaced.

'Sorry.'

'I guess it was better than being strangled by that coughing loser.'

Jesse put out one hand and hauled Chelsea to her feet.

Chelsea groaned, but managed to stand upright. 'Do you do stunt-work or something?'

'Or something,' Jesse said, dryly.

'I'm not dreaming, am I? You really hit that goon and knocked him out, didn't you?'

Jesse nodded.

'And we *did* jump from a moving train?'

Jesse nodded again.

'Cool.' Chelsea chuckled. 'Come on. It's my turn to get us into trouble.'

'What do you mean?'

'I'm taking you to meet our Gran. She'll be at the cemetery. She goes there every year on the sixteenth. It's the day you died.'

CHAPTER 41

Evelyn, Jesse's grandmother, sat on a bench, facing rows of headstones. Her hair was gray but layer-cut into a fashionable style. She had a small brown mole on her left cheek, and dark glasses covered her eyes. A thin wedding band glinted on her left hand. The wind ruffled the hem of her long skirt. Beneath it, Jesse spotted white sneakers. Sneakers with a skirt? Somehow, on Gran, it looked all right. Empty sandwich wrappers were neatly folded on the bench beside her.

If Chelsea hadn't warned her about Gran, Jesse might not have guessed straight away. Gran's head was up and she looked as though she was examining the carved words on the headstones. But she was examining her memories.

As the girls approached, Gran turned her head in their direction. 'Chelsea?'

'Yes, Gran.'

'Is it time to go home?'

'Yes, it is.'

Jesse searched Gran's face to see if they

looked alike. Despite the wide difference in ages, the family nose was undeniable. All three of them had a *ski jump*.

Gran stood up. 'Did you have fun with your friends?'

Chelsea rolled her eyes. 'That's one way of putting it, I guess.'

So much had happened that it seemed unbelievable that Gran didn't realize that Chelsea had been abducted then rescued. But it had all happened in one day.

'The tone of your voice tells me you're anxious,' said Nan.

Jesse found it difficult to breathe, as though a heavy weight pressed on her chest. She never really believed she would see her grandmother. But already, her elation was tempered by her knowledge that they would only have a little time together. Before Jesse even said *hello*, she was preparing to say *goodbye*.

'Anxious *and* happy,' said Chelsea. 'I have some news. Get ready to hear something *really* exciting.'

The bruise on Chelsea's face was deepening, and there was a cut on her lip. Jesse was relieved that Gran wasn't aware of it. Especially as her sister looked that way because Jesse had pushed her from a moving train.

'Someone is with you.'

'Can't fool you, can I?'

'No,' said Gran. 'And don't ever try. I'm blind, but I didn't come down in the last shower.'

Jesse grinned. The family resemblance

didn't stop at the nose. It was also in the smart mouth. Even Gran had it.

'Who's here?' Gran put out one hand.

Jesse stepped forward and took her grandmother's hand. It was wrinkled, but soft. Dark veins on the back of her hands resembled country roads on a map.

'You're trembling, child.' Gran put her other hand on top of Jesse's.

'Yes.'

There was a look of shocked disbelief on Gran's face. 'Your voice ... say something else.'

'I ... I don't know what to say.'

Gran swayed as the colour drained from her face. 'I need to sit down. Chelsea?' She said the name like a command, rather than a question. 'Is this ...'

'It's my sister, Autumn.'

CHAPTER 42

As they left the cemetery, Jesse's mind flashed *Autumn* like a neon sign. *I've got my own name.* And yet, she still thought of herself as Jesse. The name *Autumn* belonged to someone she didn't know.

And there were other names; her parents, Pamela and Justin, who had died in the car crash. Suspicion shot through Jesse, but she shut it out. She didn't want anything to spoil this time with her grandmother and sister. And now they were going to surprise her Grandfather, Harris. But later, when she was alone, Jesse knew she would wonder whether C2 had deliberately caused that car crash. And she also knew she might never find out.

The girls stopped to check the traffic before crossing the street. Gran walked between them, hanging on to both of them. Not just for help in negotiating the traffic, but her grip told Jesse that Gran did not intend to lose her a second time. Jesse dreaded telling her that's exactly what would happen.

Jesse was surprised to a see familiar car parked across the street.

'I'll be back in a second. I see someone I know.' She patted Gran's hand, before moving it from her arm.

Not sure whether to feel relieved or annoyed, Jesse dashed across the street towards the battered car. She made a gesture that mimicked unwinding a window.

Liam obeyed. He had matted blood in his hair.

'You look like you had a fight with a bear and lost.'

He nodded. 'I had a fight with a type of bear, but I won. Eventually.'

'Liam, I have something to tell you about who took Chelsea and me.' She had to explain, but she wasn't looking forward to his reaction.

A sad look washed over his face. 'I know. The *bear* told me.' His face hardened. 'Eventually.' He repeated his earlier word, but this time his voice was as hard as granite. 'Don't worry. Hans Faulkner has definitely *retired*.'

Jesse shivered. The way Liam said 'retired' was chilling. She didn't ask any questions. She knew she would not like his answers.

'If you're going to follow us, you might as well give us a lift.'

'Is that a limp?' He looked at her quizzically.

'Yes, but it's not like yours. It doesn't change sides. How did you find me?'

'There's a tracking device on your collar.' She recalled his playful smack on the back of her head. That put him one up on her. She had no idea he'd done it.

'Granger asked you to follow me, didn't he?'

Liam sighed. 'Yes, he did. But I would have done it anyway. You might have needed me.'

She raised one eyebrow. 'You figured it would be easier to find out what I was doing if you were *with* me, rather than following me, didn't you?'

'Uh huh. You're learning fast. One day you'll be half good at this.'

Jesse turned, cupped her hands to her mouth and called out, 'Chelsea. Bring Gran over here. My friend will drive us.'

Liam winced. 'You might have a limp, but there's nothing wrong with your lungs. How long will you need?'

'I have two hours left before Granger's deadline.'

'Mm. I guess I won't officially discover where you are for two hours then.' He looked at Jesse intently. 'Make the most of this. I'd say the score with Granger is now even. It's unlikely he'll let you see your family again.'

CHAPTER 43

Jesse stood at the window of the room she had nicknamed the fishbowl. Outside, the lights gave a pretty, sparkling look to a city that was grubby and overcrowded in daylight. She often thought that night lights were the city's way of dressing up.

'Something is troubling you,' said Jai, from behind her. 'Please let us help. We are your family.'

She turned around, her emotions whirling like a tornado. So much had happened. And it wasn't over yet. There was one big knot left in the string of her life.

Jai and Tamarind sat at the small round table, their faces set with determination.

These two *were* family. In a different way. Families were not just about blood ties. Jesse and Jai had been through a lot together. And Tamarind had once saved her life.

Jesse sighed. 'I might have murdered someone.'

Tamarind gasped. 'Don't hold back, girlfriend.'

'Might?' Jai showed no emotion.

Jesse explained the jumbled facts. That she didn't remember meeting the man on the north slope, until the flashbacks started. Hans said the avalanche was an accident and his men were there. He insisted there was no helicopter. Then she told Tamarind and Jai about the hair-slide. 'But when I got back, it was gone.'

'Mary.' Tamarind and Jai spoke at the same time.

'Maybe. I did catch her in my room and she looked guilty.'

'She *always* looks guilty.' Tamarind pushed a lock of pale hair away from her face.

'If it was Mary,' added Jai, 'She would have been following orders from the Director. I do not believe she has the intelligence for a complicated plan.'

'I *remember* stabbing that man with poison,' insisted Jesse.

'Do you remember or *think* you remember? There is a difference. Our lives are made up of our own perceptions, the way *we* see things. Those perceptions are not necessarily true. Nor are they the same as another person's.'

Jesse wondered if Jai's scrawny body would ever match his ancient mind and formal voice.

Tamarind sent Jai a look that suggested he'd be better off reading a few comics now and then.

'That is why eyewitnesses tell different stories about one event.'

'I knew that,' said Tamarind, in a voice that fooled no-one. Not even herself.

'There was a recent experiment where volunteers in a laboratory ...' Jai swallowed.

He has trouble with that word, thought Jesse. *Bad memories.*

'One after the other, volunteers in an MRI machine had their hands covered with a sheet, so they could not see them. A rubber hand was placed beside them. Someone prodded the rubber hand at the same time that another person touched each volunteer's real hand. Then they only prodded the rubber hand and each volunteer reported that they *felt* it. When the doctor hit the rubber hand with a mallet, every volunteer flinched.'

'Gross.' Tamarind grimaced.

'The MRI recorded which parts of the brain lit up during the experiment. It showed that each volunteer truly *believed* the rubber hand was their own.'

'So they were made to believe something that wasn't true,' said Jesse, thoughtfully.

Jai nodded.

'I had an MRI this morning.'

Tamarind looked stunned. 'Whoa.'

'Tell me,' asked Jai. 'What do you feel when you have these flashbacks, Jesse?'

'Nothing.' She shrugged. 'Nothing at all.'

'Ah.' Jai rested his chin on one hand. 'Our strongest memories are attached to an emotion. That is what *makes* us remember. Therefore, this problem is solved. If you did not feel any emotion, then ...'

'The memories are not mine.'

CHAPTER 44

Jesse sat, alone and cross-legged on the floor, her hands curled gently, one on each knee.

Director Granger had been clever. He had entwined false memories with things that had really happened, so they were believable. But at last, Jesse had separated the real from the pretend in her mind.

Ari, the C2 scientist who had done her upgrade, once told her that she had no idea how much more she could do because of her nanites. He said, 'You will discover these things when you are ready.'

Jesse had not given permission for the nanites to be placed in her body, but she was stuck with them. Her body was now dependent on them. If they were removed, she would go crazy, then die.

But there was one thing she *could* do. Give back what she didn't want. If C2 could use computers to send false memories to her mind, could she return them?

Grand Master Kim had said, 'Your mind is your greatest strength.'

Closing her eyes, Jesse breathed deeply.

Her pulse slowed.

She imagined her special meditation place, with its moss-covered stairs leading down to a deep pool. Hummingbirds hovered, mid-air, with their tiny heads buried in tubular flowers. There was a slight breeze. Not enough to irritate, just enough to cool her skin.

Still relaxed and in a dream-state, she drifted from the garden pool to imagine the minuscule nanites in her bloodstream. Really tried to picture them, although they were too small to see.

There. Black dots in a red stream. She sensed energy flowing back and forth, from the nanites to the outside of her body.

Jesse floated with the energy.

There was something shiny ... electrical circuitry.

She focused on the unwanted memories that had been thrust into her mind. One by one, she summoned them and imagined pushing them away from her, back into the computer.

CHAPTER 45

Jesse opened her door to frantic pounding. Granger, Mary and Michael from the lab, stood there.

'Are you all right?' Although Granger was still elegantly dressed, his cheeks were unusually pink and there was a sheen of perspiration across his forehead. 'Something strange has happened.'

'Oh?' Jesse had a pretty good idea what that might be, but she wasn't going to make this conversation any easier for him. What he had done was twisted and cruel.

'Some of our nanotechnology programs have crashed,' said Granger.

Jesse leant one hand on the doorframe. 'Wouldn't be the memory sequence, would it?'

Granger exchanged a worried look with Michael.

Mary simply looked confused. She jutted her neck forward, looking more like a cobra than usual.

'I didn't want those memories, so I sent them back,' said Jesse.

'You did *what*?' Granger's pink cheeks turned red.

He should get his blood pressure checked, thought Jesse.

'You can't do that!'

'I *can*,' said Jesse. 'And I *did*. A C2 experiment made my brain work faster. So now I'm using it. And if you fix the program and send more fake memories, I'll do the same again. Only harder.'

Granger looked like a beached fish with his bulging eyes and flapping mouth.

Jesse almost felt sorry for him. But not quite.

As she watched for his reaction, she saw his panic swept aside by cunning. Director Granger might not be a genius, but he was a wily schemer who knew when he was outplayed.

Granger smoothed down his hair with one hand, then forced his mouth into a tight smile.

'It would concern me if technology leapt ahead before we were ready for it,' he said. 'Perhaps we should shelve the memory project.'

'That's a good idea,' said Jesse, in a quiet voice. 'And I have another idea. Well, not mine exactly, but it's from someone close to me.'

She pictured Gran's face at the house. Lies took time. Secrets took trust. So Jesse told Gran the truth about her past. Not all of it, but enough so that Gran would understand.

'Why those ...' Although Gran was not a young woman any more, she knew some colorful words, and she let fly with them. Then she said, 'I've got an idea of my own.'

It was a blockbuster.

'I met my grandmother,' Jesse told Granger.

Mary shot him a look that dripped with unspoken questions and accusations.

'Gran would like to see me more often. She knows I can't leave C2, for lots of reasons,' said Jesse. 'But she'll settle for once a month, and so will I.'

'Out of the question,' snapped Granger.

'It's too dangerous,' added Mary.

'Gran's pretty stubborn. Runs in the family. We wrote down lots of things that have happened to me and sealed them in a package. If I don't show up for my visit or Gran has an *accident*, that package goes to someone she knows. That person has also chosen one other, and the line goes on for about twenty people. No-one, including Gran and me, knows everyone in the line,' said Jesse. 'But in the end, the package will go to Gran's good friend.' Jesse told Granger the name of that good friend, and he gasped.

Granger would try to find a way out of it. But it would take him some time. Jesse felt the last invisible knot untangle.

CHAPTER 46

Jesse clicked on her emails.

There was one from Rohan, who was undercover somewhere. He was okay. Good.

Liam's name popped up on the screen. She clicked on his message. *Answer: You. It's the nose.*

What did that mean? She scrolled down, following arrows. Liam had written more. *Question: Which twin is the best-looking?*

But typically, Liam couldn't be seen to be too nice. He had to add an instruction. *PS. Be ready on time tomorrow. Six am. We have a new assignment. Wear boots.*

Jesse had one email to go, and it set her heart racing. Not certain she should open it, she left it until last.

Her emails were secure. They were routed all around the world, with electronic gateways and traps.

What made her tingle was imagining what was in the message. Most of all, she didn't want her sense of anticipation to be crushed.

The slip of paper the young man at the lodge

handed her had an email address written on it. Nothing else. He could just be an ordinary guy, but maybe not. Either way, it was a risk emailing him. But one she had not been able to resist. All she knew about him was that he had dimples and his email address showed his name was Devlin.

Jesse clicked on his email and started reading.

Discover more about the dangerous
assignments of
JESSE SHARPE

Book #1: SECRETS
Jesse is assigned to protect a young girl, but
it goes dangerously wrong.

Book #2: FUGITIVE
Jesse is sent out to bring someone in to C2.
To do so, she has to infiltrate a protest group
called 'Peace First'.

Book #3: NIGHTMARE
Nimbus, a vicious shadowy organization,
have placed an agent at a children's camp.
Jesse must work out who it is and what
Nimbus plan to do.

Book #4: DANGER
Jesse has to find a hidden bomb before
thousands of people die, and time is
running out. But the threat turns out to be
more complicated and deadly than anyone
imagined.

CHRISTINE HARRIS

Christine lives in South Australia. She
has written over fifty books which have been
published in many countries.
She was nine years-old when she wrote
her first book. Although it was never
published, she considers it a triumph
because she wrote it while sitting in a tree in
her Nan's back garden.
When writing about Jesse Sharpe,
Christine became so involved in the
excitement of the story that she couldn't
sleep. 'Jesse is a wonderful character. I'd like
to be her.'
But Christine also believes, 'Everyone can
be a hero in their own life.'

www.christineharris.com

Printed in the United States
209720BV00009B/5/A

9 781595 941510